Stories From The Twisted Hairs

First Printing

ISBN number: 978-0692891629

This is a work of fiction. Any resemblance of characters to person living or dead is coincidental.

Book compiled, edited/designed by L. Teresa Whitehawk
Published by Eagle Bear Press.
printed in conjunction with CreateSpace. Printed in the United States.

Stories From The Twisted Hairs

The Storyteller

Written and Illustrated
By L. Teresa Whitehawk

Index of Stories

Index of Paintings

Introduction
Notes to the Reader

The Twisted Hairs are teachers of mixed blood Indigenous Peoples who bring together knowledge of many sources, many ethnicities, and braid that knowledge together as "braids of truth."

The original Twisted Hairs Society is believed to have begun around 1100 AD, near Oaxaca, Mexico, combining Cherokee and Tribal Mexican teachings. Among the Cherokee the word 'hair' is a symbol of knowledge and wisdom. A Twisted Hair Storyteller traditionally unbinds his hair and lets it fall loosely before beginning to tell a tale.

The painting(s) were done before the stories were in printed form and the figure of the "Twisted Hair Woman" is a mask the artist imagined for the story teller.

In some of the paintings there is a red ribbon or string. The archetype which comes from Asia of the red string, denotes separation or divorce. In the author's mind is also suggests renunciation of the world, thus the Twisted Hair assisted the individual with finding truth and self-understanding.

The author's origins come from Mexico and the United States, and like the original Twisted Hairs, she has remained hidden from the world, maintains a strong prayer life, and has passed through years of rigorous Indigenous Ceremonies. Her visions come to support her in her search for truth. She makes small paintings and stories from life experiences, following the Twisted Hair's path to truth.

The Egg Woman

Marya held tight to the child's hand as she stooped to look in the chicken's nest. Long ago when her legs had been as short as the child's own she had trembled when her mother taught her to unseat the hen and look beneath for the smooth pearl-like treasure of eggs. Her child flinched as Marya held out the tiny hand to feel these new eggs. Even though the hot summer day made an acrid ammonia smell from the chicken dung, mother and daughter lingered and marveled at the translucent orbs that lay now in the matted and dirty grass.

"Listen," she said almost secretly to the child. "If you listen quietly to the birds behind you, you will know which hen is coming toward you." She now raised the three eggs in her one hand, as deftly as a thief might have, but with much tenderness. Now it was the child's turn to marvel, seeing the three eggs, as if held by a Black magician, the creamy white and brown against Marya's black hand.

"Shh, the hen is returning." Behind them the hen strutted, indignant with clucking, lifting her feet high, moving her head back and forth considering attack, then quieting. The hen supposed she must give up these eggs to the woman.

The child took each egg gently, placing them carefully atop the other eggs already lying in the basket. The woman then stooped quickly, wiped her hand deftly against the dry grass of the last nest, cleaning herself of bits of bird droppings.

"It is time little one, that we made our way to town."

*****

Ruby leaned toward the mirror of her borrowed bedroom. She was enjoying the thought of dressing in her daughter's African bungalow, feeling rather exotic. She dressed carefully as she always did, preening hair and clothing to ensure that not one unwanted wave or wrinkle mar the thing she hoped to create. She leaned toward the mirror, pulled her lip down slightly to look at her teeth, a habitual thing with her. She muttered, "All mine."

The thought had never bothered Ruby before, but now she checked to see if wrinkles might be showing in her plump face. She reminded herself that she had waited too long to come to this country. She counted her list of places visited: Palestine, Greece, England, and Scotland. She was most determined to find the gifts she had promised herself all these years. She retrieved her can of hair spray from the cosmetic case she'd slipped down under the bed, fearful the African houseboy would pilfer these things too. Her daughter told her of Africans able to steal silently into bedrooms as White people slept, carrying off what they felt was worth money.

"Constance," she called out the door to her daughter. "I'm so glad you two could do it this year. You talked about it so long. I didn't think you would truly come to Kenya, but I'm so glad you did."

Constance stood in front of the hallway mirror for her last minute self-inspection. She dabbed on pink lipstick less carefully than her mother. "Two years seemed like such a long time to stay here, Mother. Such a long time to be away from home." She held up her hand in front of the mirror, attentive to the growing stiffness in her hands and to the slight deformity that increased in her finger joints. She could not explain rheumatoid arthritis to herself, no matter what the doctors said.

Ruby finished in the bedroom with three more pokes at her hair, like a beast that pokes too long at itself.

"I'm ready. How far is it to this village market place you told me about?"

"Five miles," Constance sighed. "We can walk part of the way if you like. It's just..."

"Oh no, Dear. The car will be fine. I can go walking when I am more familiar with the area. Perhaps the houseboy can accompany me later."

Constance put her arm around her mother and gave her a squeeze. Though affection between them sometimes lagged, after being in Africa for a long six months, Constance had been glad to see Ruby's familiar face. Now she pecked her mother's cheek as they strolled out to the car.

***

Marya hummed and swayed a little as she and small Cesily walked along the road. Marya's green-blue skirt wrapped around her hips and hugged at her ankles. She had taken to wearing the loose woven brown shirt whenever she left her small compound to cover her nakedness. Her son Jenyata had told her that it was not lady-like to walk outdoors with no clothes.

She smiled with pride for Jenyata. She missed him too much she knew, had relied on him too heavily. She smiled to see his smile in her mind's eye, him holding up the white paper that showed his good grades. His perfect English was a pride to her, and when he was home he insisted she learn the English words more rapidly than she thought herself capable of, but the new language had been of benefit to her at her egg sales.

Marya laughed aloud and sang out to her little daughter, "Ex'cellent!" She could imagine Jenyata's shining eyes, mimicked his tone. "Ex'cellent! Ex'cellent!" Cesily laughed at her gracious mother. Nothing so beautiful, nothing so excellent, thought Cesily, smiling up at her.

Marya and Cesily shaded their eyes simultaneously, looking toward the Village Square. Already marketers were busy spreading out the vegetables and fruits. Already the sun shone hot and the moisture rose from the night dampened ground.

"Unh, unh, unh," Marya hummed, then fell silent as she watched the few light-skinned people walk between the Blacks who crowded the stalls.

Marya chose a spot toward the end of the vegetable and fruits row. She always put her back toward the meat stalls, where live chickens were tied by the feet and hung from poles. She could not stand the smell of death she knew awaited them, the smell of chicken dung, hot feathers and fear. She had sold a few of her chickens over the years to buy the bits of things they needed to live, but she would never sell them directly to the people in the market. Instead she sold them to the man who stopped by her home from time to time, adding them to his own ducks and chickens which he made a fair profit from in the same market. For her own family, she preferred the eggs and vegetables, and sometimes a bit of the foreign cheese they found, though it cost a dear penny for a taste. She planned today to buy beans and cornmeal, enough to last them for the week. And something for Jenyata, who would be home for the weekend. Perhaps some dried figs, she thought. He had promised to come home, even if he had to walk the seventy miles from his father's.

Marya tugged at Cesily to sit beside her near the stalls. Cesily was quick to oblige and sat wide-eyed and listening, just as her mother did. Marya listened even more carefully than the child, for she could understand the dialects of several tribes and sat listening for news from distant places. She listened too, most carefully, to the talk of any English-speaking man who passed close enough to be heard. She heard of wars and rumblings from the people of the South. She heard other things she did not understand, how people were killed in the mines by the hundreds, and how someone, a king's man, had brought something worthless from another country and sold it to their people as if it were a thing of great worth. She heard this talk and did not understand what it meant.

Now a small car drove close to the stalls and two White women climbed out tugging at their skirts. Marya imagined the smell of their flesh as they walked to the first stall. She had talked with the slender White woman before whom she guessed to be near her same age, but so painful it seemed for the woman to walk. She walked with much more difficulty that the older woman beside her. It was this second woman that Marya could smell. Like one animal viewing another from a distance, a recognition passed through Marya that made her shiver. She had been called names before, Marya had, names meaning something like a witch, that meant the devil had touched her with a wisdom other people are afraid of. The greying, steady footed White woman would certainly call her a witch, Marya thought.

The old woman was so sure. Sure of what, Marya could not guess, but the woman moved with sureness.

There was an instant when Marya chose to stay. Her feet under her twitched to be up and gone. Her arms ached to reach out, grab her tiny daughter and flee, protecting the child by hiding it. She could see herself, basket hoisted again upon her head, child beneath her arm, fleeing toward home. Her feet twitched and she moved almost nervously. Cesily began motioning with her little hands, patted the air as if speaking about something. Marya said, "Be still. Those women will buy something from me, but the cost is too dear."

At one of the stalls closest to the road, artisans sat with their carvings of animals and Black Men Wisdom statues. Here the two White women spent some time, and Marya hoped they wanted little else, but she knew the younger woman would buy things she needed for home, and of course, the eggs would be needed too. The older woman was fat. Marya whispered the word in English a few times and then decided against it. No. Not fat. The woman was solid, but she had breasts like small pillows. Those kinds of breasts, Marya thought, in this country are for holding grand-children and pillowing them, but this woman...

The White women stood, facing the artisan who was showing his work. He rose from the ground and went to a pack he had behind his stall and brought forth a white stone carving that was worth something more than what he had been showing. It was the carving of a magician, this one pure white because of the stone, but with all the features of the Black artist who carved it. The forehead sloped like a young African's, but the eyes were hollow places, like the death masks of people Marya sometimes dreamt were encircling her. She watched the heavy woman lift the White African figure toward the sun, as if to look through it. It did have magic to it, but to Marya the white stone made it seem a too solid ghost.

She listened to the two women haggle over price with the artist, and when the dealing was done, the older woman seemed to chirp something pleasantly; this was the thing she had been hunting for.

The two women moved down the line of food goods and the younger one chose what she wanted. The older woman held the wrapped bundle tightly under her arm, as if the thing might be a stolen article and she afraid of being found out. The solid woman moved in and out of the stalls in her solid way, poking now at foods and staring unabashedly at the people around her. She chose one soft green melon as round as herself, poked and prodded it with white sharpened fingers.

All this Marya watched, and forgot to look interested in the other people in the market who might want to buy some of her eggs. She began thinking of the snake man who sometimes sat at the market. He fascinated many people into giving him pennies by dancing with his snake. Marya hooded her eyes in a way she thought the snake might do, so that when the women moved closer to her they would not be able to see into her soul.

The younger woman stepped up close to Marya. She had talked with Marya before and now wanted to show off to her mother. She pulled Ruby close beside her.

"Mother, this woman speaks English. Hello, Marya. How are you today?" said Constance.

Marya nodded respectfully, tilting the basket of eggs toward them to take attention away from herself. Constance was insistent.

"Mother, this is Marya. She is the only woman here who speaks English, and in such a lovely way too."

"Hello, Lady," said Marya, thinking determinedly to say no more.

"This is my mother, Marya. She has just come from the United States. Will you introduce your daughter to her?"

Marya nudged Cesily, not without gentleness, but with more energy than usual, which told the child to be twice as cautious as usual. "This is my daughter Cesilee," said Marya precisely. She kept her eyes turned delicately away from them. The large woman loomed down toward both of them, her odor overwhelming as Marya had imagined. A smell of light white perfume, of old woman's bloodlessness, of something that sucks air, of a time Marya could not remember, but made her breathless all the same. The woman put forward her solid hand, white and freckled, demanding. She took Cesily's little hand into her own and spoke as if looking at a monkey's miniscule hand. "Why, the child is a treasure. Look how her hand curls up in mine! And look at these eggs! I have not seen larger ones anywhere, not even in our supermarkets, Constance!"

"Of course not, Mother. People at home do not care for their animals the same way I am sure Marya does. Have you been well this week, Marya?"

"Yes, Lady," Marya nodded. She tugged at Cesily's ankle, and the child sat down immediately.

"Look to yourself," Marya said to Cesily in their own tongue, "And do not look into the light eyes of the large woman."

The two women began choosing out the perfect and largest eggs for themselves.

Marya sat more still and erect than was her usual habit, reminding herself that she had no need of the women's money, if indeed they asked her for too much. She reminded herself of the sack of rice in her hut, and the eggs.

"Constance," the older woman said, "Do you suppose this woman would mind sometime if I came to her house and visited with her?"

"Well, Mother, put the question to her; she can understand."

"Your name is...Marya? My name is Ruby. Ruby Matlock. I have come to visit my daughter and her husband while they are living here. I have always admired your people." She faltered. The Black woman seemed intractable. "I would like very much to visit you in your home. I have always been fascinated by Africa."

Marya looked up once at the younger woman, whose face was less formidable, the eyes less probing. Perhaps this younger woman knew something of privacy, but the other woman, what was she?

"I am a very poor woman," said Marya. "I have little to sell, less to cook, and I have nothing to show to anyone but these eggs themselves." She poked at the eggs now left in the basket, less careful of their goodness than she had been. "You are welcome, Lady, but there is nothing to see."

The two American women seemed pleased. "Perhaps in a week or two," suggested Constance.

"You may come tomorrow," said Marya, the decision made. She did not want to wait more than one day with the thought of these two women finding her home. They paid the highest price for the eggs without question and seemed quite glad. Marya remembered again that Jenyata was coming on the weekend and she hoped by then she would be able to sweep the place clean of the smell of these women.

She quietly drew in the dirt for them, the black of her hand shining against the rough black of the dirt. She drew for them the road by which she walked to and from town, and how they should turn before the end of the one long fence. Hers was the place nearest the grove of palm trees.

***

Marya sat at sunset inside her hut, watching the last orange sunlight stream through the doorless entry. She watched the motes of sunlight, listened to her small flock of chickens close outside her door. Cesily worked her mouth around cornmeal mush, listening to night sounds and ignoring this new mood in her mother. There were ten stones that Jenyata had brought to his sister on his last visit, which she toed about in the dirt. They were smooth, almost egg shapes. He had told her how the man who sold them polished them to fineness with sand and water.

"Mother, what is soapstone?" She asked into the gathering dark. Her mother did not turn her eyes toward the child. "Mother," Cesily said most quietly. She pulled her mother's hand out and opened the palm. She placed the smoothest and largest stone

Jenyata had given her into Marya's palm, then shut her mother's fingers around it.

"Thank you, my daughter," said the woman, and she sat holding the stone till the daylight was gone.

***

Morning chores were done long before the sun was high again in the sky. The night had passed for Marya like many nights, her only warmth the small Cesily tucked close beside her body. So many things having left Marya in her life, she knew only the joy of quietness alone, of Jenyata's noisy returns and the sense of their belonging together, and of Marya's showing bits of life to her daughter that both marveled in. The way light rose in the morning and warmed the earth, the way food came to them from a neighbor when their pots were empty, the way love returns and goes out from the house again with Jenyata's coming and going. It did not seem to matter to Marya that she could sit perfectly still in the world, moving only as far as the village and back again. She knew everything came to her, even those things which she had thought should be kept away.

She knew long before the women arrived just when they would be there. They had said afternoon and she had said morning. She had said to please walk carefully from the road, and she knew they would drive right up to her door. Jenyata had told her of some of the White people he had met, but he always said they were in some way no different than anyone he had ever met, and Marya repeated this as many times as she could in her mind. Her husband had called her a secretive woman. But her silence had not fallen on her until he had begun beating her. Her withdrawal from him had been from within, since he would withdraw from without. All things seemed so quiet to her here, no sounds of anything, except her small daughter and the birds that pecked in the yard.

She came to the doorway at noon, stood watching the road and the sunlight. She picked a piece of twig from her hair and cleaned her teeth. She thought whether to put the rough blouse over her body and decided the heat was too strong, and besides, she would dress and be herself here in her home.

The car came right up to the doorway. The two women drove the length from the road and her house as if they knew every inch of her small place. Their servant man rode in the back of the car. He seemed to be there more as a witness of things than for any real purpose Marya could think of.

The noisy motor stopped. The car jerked once. It was the color of sand. Two doors opened; two women emerged. The Black man opened the back door and unfolded as he stepped out. Marya could think of nothing to say. The chickens had scattered with the noise of the car and gathered again around Marya as she led the women to where the chickens nested. She answered their questions in one word to each question.

She walked them to the doorway of her hut and stood by while they peered in. If they should enter, she thought, I shall not know how to clean it when they are gone.

Cesily disappeared beneath a bush, leaving her round stones at the doorway of the hut. She stayed there out of sight, as if her mother had shunned her, told her to remove herself for a while. That had never happened before. Even Jenyata, whom she pestered when he was home, never shunned her.

The two women seemed interested in everything. The stone where Marya ground cornmeal to powder, the watering ditch for the chickens. When they saw Cesily's stones they asked what they were.

"Soapstone," was all Marya could say. The large woman stooped and picked them up, one by one.

"How are they made?"

"With the hands," Marya said. "they are shaped by rubbing sand and water against the stone."

"It must take a long time," said Ruby. "May I keep one?"

Marya looked directly at the old woman once and then shrugged. What could she say? The woman stood up with one in her hand, the largest one. Marya watched the white and spotted hand close around it.

Marya stepped toward the fence that marked the end of her compound. There was nothing to say but that which was closest to her heart. "My son, he is fifteen years old. He has taught me to speak English. He is in that direction. He lives with his father who now has another woman. Jenyata is my son's name, and on the Friday night, he comes home to me if he can. He is going to Secondary School. He is going to be the leader of my people when he is a man."

The two White women had much less to say than the day before. She was glad not to have to listen to the words of their mouths. She had watched their lips move closely around their words and had wondered how such sounds could mean anything, coming from such mouths.

"I am only a poor woman," Marya repeated. "I am lonely and I am poor, and I feed my little one by raising these chickens. What more?"

The women said thank you and gave her some of the money that they pay for other goods. She could not understand. They opened their purse pockets and took out coins, several of them. They put them into her hands, more than one hand could hold. They told her thank you again and again. They said they would not have to bother her again, but that they were grateful for their visit.

"Perhaps we will send you some cloth?" Ruby said. "Yes, we shall send you some cloth, or we can send you some flour. Which would you like?"

Marya did not say thank you. As she watched their car back away from her house, she asked herself aloud, "What did they come for?" Cesily crawled out from under the bush and came and stood in front of her mother.

"What did you do that for my little one? Why did you run and hide?"

"You pushed me away from you Mother," said Cesily. The salt stains on Cesily's round, delicate cheeks shown as white salt crystals. Marya bent down and lifted her high up in her arms. She swung her gently to and fro. She perched Cesily on her bare black shoulders and turned toward the sun. Walking and swinging, she hummed the soft 'Unh, Unh, Unh,' till the little girl no longer frowned.

Taming the Beasts of Passion & Ignorance

In the Land of Milk and Honey

Everyone knew who Aunt Etta Jo Claibon was. In her younger days, she had run a Ribs 'n Things Café from a small building in her backyard. She had coaxed one of her cowboy 'sons' to make an 8-foot-long grill from an oil drum for her to cook ribs. Now she had been cooking on it for more than 30 years. She kept her prices a bit lower than the neighboring restaurants and of a Friday night she always had twenty or more customers waiting for their orders.

She pocketed that money to supplement her husband's income, but the main use she put her portion to was to pay preachers to come from out of town to teach the people how to live – according to Aunt Etta's way. Often the preachers were Black men she'd seen on the Gospel cable channel. They were good-looking, dynamic, entertaining and could draw a crowd even in the 99% White town where she lived north of San Francisco.

She herself was flamboyant, nappy red-haired, and mulatto, maybe part American Indian, and married to a thin Black man who never stole the lime-light from her.

For the last ten years, she had wielded her long barbecue fork over the roasting ribs from a wheel chair, her hips gone bad and constantly aching. She did not let this stop her from her personal mission of spreading the Gospel, and her sales increased. She always put small religious flyers in with the rib orders too, reminding people they were sinners and should come to Jesus. And you can bet most of her buyers did read those pamphlets and thanked her for them as well as the tasty ribs. She added side dishes too – home cooked beans in a red sauce and home-made coleslaw with bits of apples chopped into it.

On Sundays and for social outings she knew how to dress - in long skirted expensive suits, this time a lavender colored one with a huge lavender colored hat with veil. Another time a long creamy green outfit, accessorized with a hat that made her look a foot taller, and wearing heavy and impressive African animal fetish jewelry.

She explained to me that the long, painted fingernails and false eyelashes were a necessity too. I marveled at her audacity in dress and speech. She bragged about once being fired from her job at the local hospital as a Licensed Practical Nurse. She told me how long and how difficult it had been for her to finish the course to become an LVN, and she lost her job in a moment by praying over somebody to get well who had not given her permission. The hospital where she had worked was run by Catholic nuns and she was Pentecostal, sometimes Baptist - Preacher, Healer, and Prophetess (though she often told me women were not to be the Preachers).

One day when I was at her home she had the Gospel channel playing in the background. Tammy Faye was being interviewed and Aunt Etta told me she had a great affection for Tammy Faye, whose husband ended up in jail for absconding and misusing follower's money. But Tammy Faye had been able to stay out of jail and live in high style off some of those proceeds.

"You know all that make-up and fancy fingernails and her expensive outfits are jus' her getting ready to 'work it'," Aunt Etta said.

"Work it?" How do you mean?" I asked.

"Why she's out there spreading the Gospel," Aunt Etta said.

Many people adored Aunt Etta, I think because of her enthusiasm and the flamboyant way she lived her life. I had taken to visiting her every week and found it exhausting to be with her for more than an hour. On Valentine's Day I was with her when she went to her clothes closet and pulled out every red garment and accessory she owned.

I had come to transport her to a day of Revival. She carefully adorned herself with Valentine covered socks over black net nylons with crooked seams. We live in a cool climate and she explained "Why Baby, these nylons with socks help me stay warm." She shoved her feet into red satin three-inch heels, the kind with very pointed toes. Her tailored red dress was topped with a long red coat.

Crammed in the back of the closet she found one of her silken scarves covered with big red hearts. The hat she chose was a red velveteen box type that sat on her orange-red curls in a straight and deliberate manner.

I had known of Aunt Etta for a few years. I was in an interfaith choir that sang all Black Gospel music and she had been named "Mother of the Choir." When we gave concerts, she came to give us her blessing and if she felt able, she sat in the front row and got up and danced in the aisle with her arms uplifted when a song roused her to the Spirit. On the day of the Valentine's Revival she had asked me to sing for the congregation and to transport her to and from the daylong event. She complained to me "I wish I'd brought my own car so I wouldn't have to wait around for you while you're visiting with folks."

"I won't make you wait for me," I promised. But after the gathering was over it was me tapping my foot waiting almost an hour while she hugged and greeted a host of people. I did not complain.

"I was born in Texas!" She bragged to the couple who came to shake her hand. "Right in the town of Lubbock, in the Panhandle! Everything IS bigger in Texas, except for the Panhandle!" She ended her sentence in a high squeal that made several people turn and stare.

In her very pointy three-inch high heels she could hardly walk, so whoever was standing closest to her would offer an arm for her to wobble forward, her gait emphasizing her bowed legs. She had to stop often, sit down often, and fan herself with a paper program.

Up until my boyfriend came to live with me I had only seen her at music events, never been up close and personal. By the time he came to town Aunt Etta was approaching her 80th birthday. We met her in the parking lot of the Winco Store as we were coming out and she was going in.

"Oh, there you are Miss Trish! Who's dis nice little man here?" She had renamed me Trish because she said she could not pronounce my name Cherise.

"This is my boyfriend Edward Dee," I said. "He's from Texas too, Aunt Etta."

"He is?" She drawled sweetly. "Well, what town you born in, Honey?"

Eddie responded, "From Tornado Alley – a tiny town called Slaten. Ever heard of it?"

Aunt Etta seemed to glow. "Why, yes, I know that place. And you're a down right nice little man. You her sweetheart then, yes?"

It was the week before Thanksgiving. Eddie was carrying a pumpkin under one arm; I was under his other arm. Eddie blushed a little and he and I hung on to one another. It felt like we were holding one another up.

"Well, right now I'm invitin' the both of you to come to my house for Thanksgiving Dinner, you hear! You don't bring nothing! I have a table full o' people come around and I fix everything! There'll be turkey in cornbread dressing, ladyfingers with banana cream pie, and of course punkin pie. I make 30 punkin pies to sell every year, but I'll save some for us – and a sweet potato pie too!"

During the week, I tried to fill Eddie in about Aunt Etta. "I heard she's not much of a housekeeper," I said. "She said her husband was the tidy one, before he died. I guess he had a heart attack a few years ago. He always worked out at the sawmill – the only Black man employed by the company. He left her with their house and a decent pension."

"She sure reminds me of the old Baptist ladies back home," Eddie said.

Come Thanksgiving night I opted for bringing her flowers, a bouquet of huge sunflowers with no vase heavy enough to hold them up. I put them in a ceramic crock-pot and Eddie and I climbed the few steps up to her porch. The two-story house was freshly painted a deep burgundy color, trimmed with a slate blue. The porch was hugged by an over grown collard greens bush that overtook the railing. I knew we'd have collards cooked with ham hocks too.

The front door opened directly into the living room, and as Aunt Etta Jo opened the door to us I could see the room was full of people of all colors.

"Welcome you two love birds!" she said loudly. Come on in and fin' yourself a spot! Turkey's almos' coming out now!" She retreated back toward the kitchen where two women assisted her bringing in the food.

The living room was long and narrow, more than thirty feet to the other side. There was a daybed under a window at the end closest to us that was covered with dolls and stuffed animals. Two worn sitting chairs flanked the daybed. The rest of the room was taken up by the table - erected just for the

Thanksgiving Feast. It looked a bit rickety, with saw horses holding up a long heavy piece of plywood in the center and card tables set up at each end. The whole of it was covered with several vinyl plastic table coverings in Thanksgiving and Christmas motifs. The table was decorated with pillar candles interspersed with fruit, gourds and pumpkins that guests had brought. Places were set with flowered paper plates and orange plastic ware. A huge punchbowl was at one end with a mixture of orange soda and floating ice cream chunks. A thin Black woman I'd seen at choir performances was serving up cups of the concoction.

In one of the sitting chairs an over-weight middle-aged White man, poorly dressed in worn brown corduroy pants and jacket, sat crocheting on what looked to be a cap.

As Aunt Etta came back into the room she gestured to the man saying, "This here's Harold. You might want to look at the hats he's makin'. That's how he buys his food."

She introduced us around the table. "Now all you folks treat Trish and Eddie real nice! They's my new best friends!" Eddie and I looked at each other with some surprise, but I was sure she meant it. Folding chairs were shoved under the sides of the makeshift table and as we took our places we struggled not to bump into the guests seated next to us. A woman named Irene was at my right and Eddie was at my left.

There were fifteen people in the room, and Harold was still sitting in the side chair working on his crochet. He didn't look up until Aunt Etta yelled at him, "My Lord, Harold! Whatchyou doing? Get up and git over here right now!" He pulled the cap off his head that he'd forgotten he had on until then. His rumpled brown hair looked like it hadn't been washed in some time. Aunt Etta started a prayer, still impatient with him. "Lord, see dis man here with the cap in his hands! He didn't come ready for the feast!" She seemed so angry for a moment I thought she was going to put a curse on him. The young Black girl at her side put an arm around her to help her steady herself. Aunt Etta stopped, looked toward heaven and the ceiling. "Oh, No, Lord! That's not the right prayer. We're here to give you thanks and to GLORIFY your NAME!" The moment was saved and she sighed deeply.

We all turned our attention to her helpers bringing in a huge turkey on a metal tray. The cornmeal dressing was on the outside of the well-done bird, crusted over and looking like a ceramic covering. A whole baked ham was brought in with pineapple slices on top. Then cooked vegetables came in, steaming hot, with the collards in a large bowl, swimming in juices. The smells were good, wafting up and down the table. Someone brought out Martinelli's carbonated fruit juices, handing us each a glass to toast the festivities. The room was very warm with the oven having been on all day and so many people crowded into the room, the walls were sweating. I could see moldy water spots in the old wallpaper showing through. Aunt Etta looked exhausted and quite red in the face as she sat down, and Harold seemed to grow more pale as he sat at the end of the table.

That day was the beginning of a seven-year long association for Eddie and me with Aunt Etta. I've asked myself what was the great attraction we had at first to Aunt Etta? I believe it was the Tough Mother figure she portrayed. Self-centered at all times, selfish and attentive to her own needs while she generously spread her Gospel grace around. Both Eddie and I lacked those tough character traits and recognized that we sometimes needed them. I am usually kind and soft spoken but through the years, I've had friends who insulted, belittled and ignored me and I patiently put up with them until one day, I'd had an over dose of being bullied and walked away from them. I didn't know how it would end with Aunt Etta.

I would go visit her every couple of weeks to see if she was doing okay, stopping by on my way home from work. Though she still cooked her ribs and sold them from her large kitchen, she did not always look well. While I was in her kitchen one day I looked out the back windows that opened over her back yard. You could see the wooden fence had fallen in and she said she had no funds to fix it. One could see into the alley and out towards the Bay.

"Some man stopped by today and asked me if he could park his ole car in my back yard!" She complained. "I tol' him surely not! I asked him if it was stolen. Don't want the police thinkin' I'm hiding no unregistered vehicles!"

I responded, "They wouldn't think that, would they Aunt Etta?"

"No, they would not. They be my friends. They stop by to see how I'm, doin' and onct in a while I give them a taste of my ribs. They asked me what I put on them to make them so tasty. Why, it's my secret rub, I tells 'em. Nobody gets to know what's in that rub! One of these days I'm gonna patent it, you know!"

I never challenged her or argued with her, just listened. She seemed always to have so much to tell.

She loved her potted plants, which were all crowded into the kitchen atop the large butcher's block in the center of the room. There was a rubber tree plant that stretched to the ceiling, with various side stems dropping toward the floor. A 'pregnant plant' had baby plants hanging from every leaf, dropping to the floor and trying to take root in the aging linoleum. Someone had given her a white Phalaenopsis orchid, which was blooming in the center of several other plants and it kept blooming for several weeks. The kitchen was warm and steamy, not unlike a green house. She used the edges of the butcher's block for food preparation, but never moved the plants around. The room was always untidy and looked as though it needed a thorough cleaning.

It was dusk and she stood in a corner by the back door. She looked out the small window and saw the evening stars begin to shine in the darkening sky.

"This is when I feel mos' like an Injun," she said softly. "Looking out there at God's creation, looking up into His heavens… I can see clear into eternity."

Aunt Etta had plenty of health problems and aches and pains. By then she'd had a hip replacement and it had given her back her ability to walk, but she had daily pains and pills to match. Her doctors gave her the prescriptions for extra strength Norco – Tylenol with codeine. She was generous with those and offered to share them, but I declined. She also had diuretics and diabetes medications, but she often did not medicate herself properly and I was unsure when her blood sugar was high.

Eddie didn't have a job most of the first year he lived with me. He was a computer man and didn't know how or where to look for a job in our small town, not knowing many people. Aunt Etta decided he needed her help so she called him on the phone. "Eddie Dee, will you come on over an' help me fire up my barbecue on Thursday?"

"I'll do it," I heard him say, but after he hung up he said to me, "I don't know how long I can stand to be around her. She starts telling me how to live and I get very nervous. I start feeling claustrophobic...like I can't get away from her."

The next Thursday I kissed him on the cheek, wished him luck as he went out the door.

I stopped by a few hours later and found them standing before a roaring fire in her oil drum grill at the side of her house. The flames were reaching up high and the grill was under the overhanging eave.

"Is that safe?" I asked Eddie. He nodded and pointed to the nearby hose on the ground, there in case of emergency. Aunt Etta stood by in her housedress and apron, her red and greying fuzzy hair pushing out from under a cap, wielding a long barbecue fork in one hand and spatula in the other.

"Soon as the fire dies down we'll put on the ribs!" She yelled over the roar of the fire. She pointed to the side porch where three large boxes of full racks of beef and pork ribs waited. Two people walked past her front fence, gawking at the fire. She hollered at them, "Come back tomorrow! The ribs will be ready!"

Eddie looked pretty stressed and later when he came home I rubbed his shoulders. "That woman drives me crazy!" He said. "She talks nonstop and bosses me around like she owns me!"

"I know, Honey. You don't have to help her. She can find somebody else."

"She gave me a $20 bill for a full day's work. She said she'd give me $40."

In spite of his upsetness he continued to help her every week for another 3 months, until he found a part-time job as a computer tech.

When Aunt Etta finally had Medicare, and had had a hip replacement, she still had her husband with her. She told me she'd come through all the tests and surgery with flying colors because she had her husband and all her "children" praying for her.

"Don't you know, child, I have many childrens even though I never had a baby? I been knowin' the people 'round here for 40 years. They bring their little children to me for bible stories, an' I take 2-3 of them to church with me ev'ry Sunday. I am their Grandma and their Prophetess!"

She and I were sitting in her living room alone at dusk. I studied the old peeling wallpaper and how the light filtered through the yellow rayon curtain over the daybed and the stuffed toys. She sat in the side chair with her feet looking swollen in worn low-heeled black shoes. She propped them up on a low stool.

"It was strange to me how I got my walkin' back" she said. "And then the Lord jus' up and took my husband. James had helped me through the whole thing, and then it was like the Lord was tellin' me, "You has to walk on your own now." It was a harsh time for me. James and I been together more than 30 years." She fell silent and we sat quietly together.

"You know I been called to preach and teach the dope addicts 'round here don't you? Me and James – we used to enjoy a joint together when we first moved here. We met down in San Fran-cis-co.

When I was young I was quite good lookin'. I moved up from Texas to where my cousins lived in the Bay area. I used to have five sugar daddies too - all at the same time! Did you know that?"

I was kind of shocked, maybe just amazed at her, but she continued her story.

"Why, yes, I had five sugar daddies. They loved me so much! They bought me clothes and took me out to fine restaurants, and one of them, he was an old man, even paid for my motel room. I was livin' high on the hawg!"

"How did you come to move up here?" I asked her.

"Well, James and I wanted to get married, see? And I knew I wanted to live a Christian life, and I knew I had to change things, I mean CHANGE things. We put all our money together, got in our car – did you know we had a big ole pink Cadillac back then? It was a brand new pink Cadillac. We packed in all our goods, I even cooked fried chicken in a 'lectric skillet so's we'd have good food to eat on the road, and off we went! Sight unseen, we said "Eureka or Bust!" and we kept driving till we found our Land of Milk and Honey!"

"You know I be worrying about you and Eddie," She said. "About you livin' with your Honey in sin."

I sighed. "He's been with me a year and just got a job, and I'm not sure how this whole thing goes, if it's going to work out or not."

"But you a Christian lady, Trish. You cain't be living like this my child. I know he's not one of them masculine he-men, but he's good and kind."

"He has some pretty serious health issues you know," I said. "Diabetes and thyroid disease, and he won't go to the doctor and won't take his meds – even when I ask."

"Then you hands them pills to him every day, Trish. A man will do what you say if you do it that way. He'll eat just what you put in front of him too. Don't you know that?"

I sighed again, thinking of Eddie's stubbornness, and Aunt Etta's, and how to get out of the conversation.

"If you don't wants to marry him, you oughtta be telling him to get out of your house! Besides, anything happen to him, you'd be better off married to him."

"What do you mean?" I asked. "How would I be better off?"

"I'm not sure. But I be prophesying now. C'mon, let's join hands and say a prayer."

It was like she planted a seed in my brain and it took root, me thinking about whether to tell him to go or to stay. I thought about it for two weeks, wanting the decision to be my own, not hers. I knew she had manipulated my thinking, but I had been concerned that he wasn't working much and that his health was fragile.

While he was out doing an errand, I packed up part of his clothes in his suitcase and set it out on the front porch. When he came back and got to the front door he looked shocked.

"What's this for?" He asked, standing in the open doorway.

"I'm thinking it's too hard for me to keep supporting you. You need to get a full-time job or move out." I felt odd saying it, but I had made a decision.

"Give me a couple of days. I'll call my sister to come pick me up. I'll pack up the rest of my stuff." He was so compliant, no argument, no anger. Maybe he was expecting me to ask him to leave. I was surprised.

His sister arrived late the next day, driving one of those long RVs. There was enough room in that thing for all his belongings and still room for 4 people to live. He moved things out very energetically. I watched with a sinking feeling. He looked like he wanted to go. Within an hour, the goods were packed. He jumped in; they turned the huge RV around and left without him turning back to even look at me. I was devastated.

It was my decision, I thought. But then again, was it? Was it what I really wanted? It took me another two weeks for me to realize that I really cared for him and didn't want him out of my life. I had talked to him on the phone several times. His sister had helped him find a job with a grocery supplier she knew. He was already working!

"If you come back here, Eddie, will you get a job now?" I asked.

"I was looking for a computer job, you know that. I never found one. But yes, I could do something else."

I drove to the L.A. area and picked him up. While I drove, I thought of Aunt Etta, how she'd planted the idea in my brain of marry him or let him go, and why did I do pretty much what she'd said. My stomach churned. I felt like an idiot for being so weak.

When I arrived at his sister's house, Eddie and I hugged like we had thought we'd lost one another forever.

At home again he found a job quickly taking care of a disabled man. He didn't like being a caretaker instead of a computer tech, but he didn't mind helping someone and we both felt better with him contributing to the household. I never told Aunt Etta that I'd put him out of my house. I didn't want her to know. It was like she'd handed me a two-edged sword and I had hurt myself as much as Eddie – but then again, he'd gone out and found a job soon as he came back.

After this we didn't go out much. After work each day Eddie and I were content to be at home with one another. Sometimes, when I'd be fixing dinner in the kitchen I'd have radio music on and Eddie would come in, hold me very close, and dance me around.

As winter came on the rains began and it had been a steady downpour for two days and nights. Aunt Etta would not go out driving in the rain. She called and asked me to bring her some groceries.

As we put things away in the kitchen she started, "Jesus said a man and woman should <u>cleave</u> to one another, Trish! You should never get divorced."

I had already been through divorce and I wondered where she was going with this pronouncement.

"What if your husband doesn't treat you right, Aunt Etta?" I said. "What if he hits you?"

She answered me back with, "Some women think their man doesn't love them lest he strikes them. Did you know that?" After a pause, she added, "But that ain't me!"

She continued in a subdued voice, "When my Mama was dying she was still living down in Texas. I got on the Greyhound Bus and went down to take care of her. She was so sick, but I stayed right with her, for a full year.

I heard my James had a girlfriend and that he and his friends were hangin' out in my house partying all the time. And I was over there in Texas grievin' as my mother was dying!

I waited with her 'til she passed away, but Lawd, I was so angry when I came home! I cleaned house, you bet, and those boys and their Mary Juana got swept out.

You know, long time ago I had asked James for a special little handgun for me, small enough for me to carry in my purse. I still have it somewhere's in this house.

When I returned to my home and cleared the folks outta my house, I heard he was still messin' around with that girlfriend.

One day after I'd been back awhile I was just sitting in this here rocking chair. He was upstairs in the spare bedroom. He came down here and tol' me he wanted a divorce.

You want's <u>What</u>? I said to him. How can you be askin' <u>me</u> for a divorce?

He went back upstairs and I sat there, my purse in my lap. I was so angry. I put my hand in there and got out that pretty little pearl handled gun and held it for a long time. I held it up like I was gonna shoot it! I pretended I was pointing it at him!

I was so angry I started prayin', "Lord, I want to go up there and jus' pop him in the head with this gun! He wants a De-vorce! "I sat there a long time Trish, till the Lord made me calm down! Lordy, I could have shot him dead."

She fell quiet for a minute and then said with finality, "Once you marry it is 'Til Death Do You Part.'"

Aunt Etta's house had a story of its own. Some folks said she was a hoarder with every nook and cranny full of things, many of the things old now, maybe worthwhile as antiques, she'd kept them so long. Her view was much different. "Some people thinks I'm crazy," She told me. "But I have the belongin's of three different dead people, plus my own stuff. I keeps 'em here so those people will talk to me. You remembers Mary, my English friend? She used to sit beside me at every revival and Gospel Music concert. I nursed her while she was dying'. She laid in this here very daybed. She still talks to me. We were so close. And those boxes in the corner over there." She gestured to the other end of the living room. "James' favorite clothes are in my bedroom closet. The res' of his stuff is right there. He comes whenever I calls him. And the other stuff, I still has my Mama's long fur coat and some of her jewelry. I miss her so much sometimes I jus' sit and cry. She nursed me till I was six years old."

Sometimes what she shared with me would mystify me and I would think about it for days, trying to understand.

"You know, my Mama worked for the town judge in Lubbock. He was a nice man. He had one daughter, a couple years older than me. He'd give my Mama all his girl's hand-me down clothes. I always dressed real nice."

"But what about your daddy?" I asked. "What did your mama tell you about your daddy? You're part White, aren't you?"

"I'm part Injun too," She replied. "My Mama tol' me that, but she never tol' me who my daddy was...but I was real smart in school. I was a good reader, but I al'ays got in trouble. You know me, I say what I think! I almost hit a teacher lady one day. She was treatin' me real bad and I tol' her to stop or I'd hit her!"

In the corner of the living room by the front door sat an old aquarium. It was at least six feet long and empty now of water. A selection of men's ties were thrown over the long front side, and on the short side, leaning against the glass in different poses and states of repair, was a selection of aging Barbie dolls, some missing an arm or leg. Most of them were blond, some brunette, and one olive skinned one that looked Native.

"Can I have that Injun Barbie?" I asked her. I intended to take it home, redress it in Native style, and give it back to her on her birthday.

Inside the aquarium was a long plastic floral display looking faded and dust covered. I often, when left to myself, studied the things I could see in the room, adding to my memory things I had missed before. I memorized the greasy and wet spots in the wallpaper and how adjacent walls had different floral patterns and colors. You could see where a picture of Jesus had hung and then been moved over several inches. The former spot still had a nail at the top of it in a light-colored rectangle the same size as the picture.

Someone had given Aunt Etta some old nickel colored tableware. Several forks, two spoons and one dinner knife.

"I seen a mobile at the fair," she said, "made with old silverware. I'm gonna make me one of those with an old wire hanger." Sure enough, a few weeks later when I visited she had her "mobile" ensconced on the wall on the opposite side of the door from the aquarium. The utensils each hung from their handles, the knife dangling from the center.

"I got Harold to drill them holes in the silver ware," she said. "It was a lot of work for such a simple thing, but I likes it."

There was an old Victrola on the side of the front door nearest the sitting chairs and just below it was a pile of different items. New high heels in a shoe box that Aunt Etta had just bought, a wrapped present she hadn't opened yet, and a Black doll lying in an open gift box. She lifted it out and said, "People don't know it, but it used to be a real insult to be giving a Black person a Black doll. Makes us think about slavery, but look at this baby. She's got such a fancy dress - and tiny socks and shoes! But what I likes best is her red hair all done up in ringlets!" She held the doll up by her face and said, "Ain't we *cute*? Don't we look like twins?"

On another day she asked me to stop by to help her find something. That is when I saw that her bedroom was a miracle in reverse. The regular-sized doorway looked much too narrow to have brought the bed through it. The bed took up almost two thirds of the room

"It's a California King-sized bed! Ain't it a beauty?" she said.

I think I squinted up my eyes. I could hardly see the bed for all the things piled on it.

At the head of the bed nearest the door you could see a space where she slept. One of those large pillows with arm cushions was pushed up again the wall. Several bed pillows leaned against it. The shape of a body nest extended from there, just enough room for Aunt Etta to lie down. I could see there was a green damask bedspread that showed under and between piles of books. A worn Bible lay atop those. Piles of clothes, dresses, skirts and shoes were layered and lined up at the foot of the bed. An addressed cardboard box, still unopened, sat across from the corner where she slept. I could see other bits of letters and things scattered through the clothes and books. It reminded me of detritus cast up on the shore of the beach, driftwood, small stones, seaweed and crab shells.

The wallpaper in this room was faded slate blue. There was no dresser, but a long metal shelf was along the wall across from the foot of the bed. More things were on the floor than on the shelves. Lingerie, clean and dirty, was strewn across the floor. The doorless closet was perpendicular to the shelves and was so full of dresses and dress suits that it looked like nothing more could be squeezed in there.

Throw rugs were crumpled and looking hazardous as I stepped further into the room. I stepped carefully over them, straightening a couple of wrinkles out with my foot.

"Do you really need these rugs here, Aunt Etta?" I asked.

She ignored my question and said, "I lost my check book in here this morning. Help me find it. It's here somewheres."

I sat carefully on the edge of the bed and started sorting through things. There was a lot of stuff in there. I found bills, opened and unopened, a couple of pens, a brooch she said she'd lost, a banana on a plate, an extra set of keys. No checkbook.

"See Trish, this is my filing system. Everything I want or need is right here."

I nodded, speechless.

"See, this is why I shall never live in a care home. I have all my own stuff right here and I lives the way I likes. That's the way it should be!"

As seasons changed there were often cardboard boxes sitting on the porch with holiday decorations piled up, waiting for Aunt Etta to put them on the outside of her house. But one November there was no Thanksgiving at her house. When I stopped to visit, the front windows were dark. Four or five cats were roaming around on the porch looking for bits of cat food. She had taken to feeding all the stray cats in the neighborhood, cats that people abandoned when they moved away and then the strays had kittens. She had helped the local Humane Society by catching them in live cages, then the cats were taken away to be spayed and neutered. They were returned to her to live out their lives. The agency had given her a huge bag of cat food that sat inside the front door, leaning against the Victrola.

Each day she would pour new water in an unwashed huge bowl, and she'd scoop out cat food and throw it out on the porch like chicken feed. The cats would come running. If a cat became aggressive and tried to enter the living room she would shove it with her foot saying, "Oh no you don't. You stayin' outside!"

She had entrusted me with a house key by then, "Just in case," she'd said, and up until that day I hadn't used it.

"I don't give my key out to just anybody," she had said.

I knocked on the door with my knuckles and yelled, "Aunt Etta, you in there?" Then I used the metal doorknocker, but couldn't raise an answer. I repeated myself a couple more times, a little louder each time, listening for a response. Finally, I unlocked the door and shoved it open, yelling one more time. I could hear her now calling feebly from behind a cloth curtain door covering. In the cooler weather, she had put up the curtain on the doorway from the living room to the kitchen to retain heat.

"Aunt Etta?" I said, and pulled the curtain back. It was much warmer in the kitchen. I could see the oven was on and the oven door stood open to heat the room.

In the short hallway toward the bedroom I stepped carefully over the scatter rugs lying in small heaps. There was an acrid smell of urine and it was evident she couldn't get out of bed.

"Aunt Etta?" I said again. She lay against the pillows in the corner of the gigantic bed looking small and sallow. "What's going on here, Aunt Etta? How long have you been down like this?"

"Jus' a couple a days, Trish. I didn't want to bother nobody. I been too sick to get up and make my dinner. You wanna open a can of chicken noodle soup for me? I think I could eat some now."

I listened to her raspy breathing, felt her head for fever, then went into the kitchen. I came back and asked, "Do you have to have the oven on and the door open? It's kind of dangerous."

"Oh, Trish, don't you go worrying about me. The Good Lord protects me through everything, don't you know? I been using the oven that way for years."

After I heated her soup and scrounged around for saltines I took them to her.

"I think you have pneumonia, Aunt Etta. I think you'd better see a doctor right away."

"I'm okay now. See, I be sitting up and you are feeding me. I'll be better bye and bye. You can go now Trish. This is all I need."

"Are you sure, Aunt Etta?" I could take you down to Urgent Care or over to the hospital."

"Yeah, I'm sure. But maybe would you stop at the store for me? I don't have no bread. I'd love a bit of toast and jam."

"Oh, course I will. But will you promise me you'll call your doctor in the morning?"

She agreed and I went off to the store, which was only three blocks away. It took me not more than 15 minutes to find what she'd asked for. I was shocked when I arrived back at her house and an ambulance was parked in front of her doorway. She was strapped in and sat slightly propped up on a gurney. An EMT man was at the head of the gurney and another at the foot as they eased her down from the porch.

"See Trish, I told you I know how to take care of myself. These nice gentlemen are taking me to the hospital. Now you go on home and I'll be fine."

A week and a half later she was home again and feeling much better. She could still drive but was feeling weak. She asked me to take her to the doctor's office for a follow up.

As she settled into the passenger seat of my car she said, "I'm thinking I needs to go down to San Francisco."

"You mean drive yourself?"

"How else can I get down there? I ain't takin' a bus. My niece and her grown kids live down there. They're needing a visit."

"You don't look strong enough yet, Aunt Etta."

In the doctor's exam room the doctor was very officious. He checked her lungs and pronounced, "They are much clearer, but not completely yet. Are you coughing much?"

"Why, no sir, doctor. Not coughin' much at all," Aunt Etta said.

I asked him, "Do you thinks it's advisable for her to be driving down to San Francisco?"

"I don't know about that." He said. "Give it a few days and I think she'll be fine." He left the room for a moment to retrieve something.

Aunt Etta looked at me sideways and said strongly, "You think you smart, don't ya Trish. You wanted him to tell me not to be drivin' down there."

I nodded and didn't say anything more.

After that I didn't want to talk to or listen to Aunt Etta. I didn't stop in to see if she was okay. I was so distressed at being worried about her and then being talked to as if I were a child. "Oh well," I heard myself say. I had once worked with a woman who would always say, "Oh well!" whenever things didn't work out for her. For me this was an impasse and I repeated "Oh well!" when I thought of Aunt Etta.

Two months later Aunt Etta called me in tears.

"What's wrong Aunt Etta? What's happened to you?"

"I can't pay my cable bill and they shut it off! I can't get the Gospel Channel now! I don't know what to do!"

I felt like a sucker, but I knew how much that meant to her. "How much is the bill?" I asked.

"It's only $35 dollars, but I just don't have it!"

"Yes, I know. I think I can cover it this time."

So we began again. Somehow I felt like I was on a merry-go-round and she was at the stop and go lever. I paid the bill.

"Oh, Thank you Trish. I'll never forget your kindness to me. You jus' don't know how much this means to me."

The next Christmas I passed by her house and saw there were no Christmas lights or decorations on her porch. I wondered what was wrong with her. I went to the front door and knocked and heard her saying, "Come on in." She was sitting in one of those side chairs slumped over. Her skin was yellowish even in the dim light. "What's going on, Aunt Etta?"

"I'm jus' doing poorly Trish. Don't feel good and don't want no Christmas."

"I think you're depressed Aunt Etta. Could Eddie and I come over and put up a few decorations for you?"

"If you wants to, Trish. I wouldn't mind."

We took her a small tree, dug around up in the spare room and found lights and a few decorations. Once we got them all up she kind of perked up, sat straighter in her chair. I made her tea and we sat with her by the Christmas tree.

"It does make me feel better, Trish. Thank you, Trish and Eddie. I really loves you."

Six months later Eddie and I started south on a long holiday weekend. We both took a couple days extra off from work and planned to see our grown children in Los Angeles. We'd traveled this highway before and were very quiet as we took turns driving. Somewhere near Salinas we blew a tire.

We called the insurance company's emergency number and sat at the roadside and waited. There were tall Eucalyptus trees to give us shade. An old rusted factory was on the other side of the fence. The grass was tall and dragonflies flitted around us constantly.

"Did we give them the right coordinates?" Eddie asked.

"I'm pretty sure of it, Honey. But it's been almost an hour now."

We called again, the company said someone was on the way, but another half-hour and no one came. While we sat there we reminisced.

"How long we been together now?" I asked.

"Almost a year and a half," Eddie said. "Should we talk about marriage now?"

We'd already considered it and I had convinced him that I needed him to take better care of his health; he'd gone to the doctor, started taking his meds regularly. He still drank soda and smoked every day, but I knew he was trying.

"Let's ask your son if he would let us get married in his back yard," he said. I called my son and Eddie called his sister in Buena Park who had a minister's license and she agreed to do the deed. By the time a Highway Patrol car drove up we had made the arrangements. All we had left to do was to get a marriage license.

The Highway Policewoman who stepped out of her car was no more than five foot one. Eddie looked down at her feet.

"You have the smallest feet I've ever seen!" He said.

"Sure do!" Said the officer. "I have to wear children's sizes." The three of us laughed. She checked our car over and asked our names. She got us to a repair shop in Gonzalez, California - a place so small that there was no post office.

Back in the car Eddie asked, "So you really want to go through with it?"

I smiled. "It's better than going to Las Vegas, and we don't have to invite a bunch of people or explain anything to anybody."

One of Eddie's close friends took pictures. The best one was Eddie and me looking into each other's eyes with devotion just before we kissed. I got that one enlarged and made a few copies.

A month later I took a photo to Aunt Etta.

"Did you do it?" She squealed. "You really got married?"

"Of course, Aunt Etta. We do love each other. I brought you this picture." I handed over our 'sweetheart' picture.

"I'm gonna hang it right on the wall over my bed, so's I can look at you two every day! Bless you and Eddie, Trish! Bless you!"

Aunt Etta decided I needed to learn to cook Southern style to keep Eddie happy. Whenever I stopped to see her she'd give me a cooking lesson.

First it was pan fried corn bread, mixed from scratch. For this she used a small cast iron frying pan on low heat. I watched as she carefully oiled and nurtured the pan till she felt the dough was cooked enough.

"You gotta watch for jus' enough bubbles to rise, then you flip it in the pan with a flick of your wrist...like this!"

She expertly jerked the pan back once and I watched the corn bread flip upside down. She clicked her tongue at her success and watched it finish cooking.

During the next visit, she taught me how to deep fry pork chops. It wouldn't do for me to tell her Eddie wasn't supposed to eat things cooked in so much fat, so I just watched. Everything she showed me I did try at home, but I failed when I went to flip the cornbread and it landed in a mixed heap of dough on the edge of the pan. Eddie laughed with me at my attempt.

Eddie never told me whether he felt okay or not. Once in a while I could tell his blood sugar was too high. He'd come in and ask me to hold him like he was afraid of something, but he wouldn't say what. He discovered he could keep his blood sugar down by eating peanut butter and saltine crackers.

He took that for his lunch every day. It didn't sound right to me so I made sure his meals at home were balanced.

He didn't tell me about the day he fell unconscious. He was with a mechanic friend of ours and they were changing the oil in Eddie's truck. Much later our friend told me about it.

"He was leaning against the car while I was draining the oil," our friend said. "Next thing I knew, he was lying in a heap. I crawled out from under the truck and sat him up. Eddie said to me, "Man, something made me dizzy! Don't worry. I think it's just my blood sugar." Our friend said, " I thought maybe that's what happened when your blood sugar went high, but I don't know much about diabetes."

I didn't hear about that incident until Eddie fell again.

It was Friday morning and Eddie was running late getting ready for work. He rushed through the room, kissed me lightly on the cheek, and went out the door.

Fifteen minutes later the neighbor woman came banging on the front door. She was breathless and said, "My husband fell, my husband fell!"

I ran out the door with her to help her, but when we approached the fallen man, it wasn't her husband – it was Eddie. I looked at her in confusion.

Her husband was still sitting in their small red Datsun in the passenger seat.

"We already called 9-1-1," the woman said, then she ran and got in the car and drove away with her husband.

Eddie had fallen on the pavement, right beside his truck. I knelt down beside him and saw he was already turning blue. But I felt his hand and his chest and his body was still warm. I gave him a kiss on the forehead and knew it was cool, and then started to try mouth to mouth resuscitation. There was something in his mouth and I tried to clean it out. I heard sirens getting closer.

The emergency crew took over. I stood aside and knew he was already gone. They did CPR and then electric shock. They loaded him into the ambulance and left for the hospital, which was 3 miles away. I drove right behind them.

I stood in the ER while technicians worked to revive him. When they pounded his chest, I felt like they were beating him up. But the monitors did not show any movement. He did not awaken. The doctor stood beside me, pronounced him dead, and said he believed it was cardiac arrest.

It was such a shock to me that when I got home I sat in a stupor except for when I was calling relatives. I felt numb and could not believe he was gone. About two days later when I felt a little more sensible I called Aunt Etta and told her what happened.

She howled into the phone. "Oh, I'm so sorry Trish! I'm so sorry!"

The phone call was brief, but before we hung up she said, "Trish, I can't be with you at the funeral. I'm sorry! It hurts too much. I can't watch all this. I'm sorry for that too!"

I remember that Eddie and I had shared the movie, "As Good As It Gets" two nights before he died and we laughed at the two people loving each other but fumbling, making mistakes with each other at every turn. I couldn't watch it again. After his burial, my grief changed into a different numbness. I started buying videos and watching movies every night. Then I would go to the library and take out a stack of their videos every week.

A few weeks later Aunt Etta called me.

"Trish, will you come and sing at my new revival? I really need you!"

"Sure, yes," I said numbly to her. I could do it one more time.

"I'll put you right up on the stage so all the people can hear you!" she said.

"Yes, I'll do it," I said. I could hear my voice was very flat.

Aunt Etta had been widowed about ten years. She had told me before that "After a while you get to wanting to be with a man again." She had taken up with a man she had known for a long time, a preacher, a Texan and a White man. He had buried two wives that had died of cancer. He was looking for another wife. When I'd speak to her all she could talk about was this man and how interesting he was. He was 76 years old. He had told her, "I know you used to be looking at me. You wanted to be with me, didn't you?" Maybe he was right. He was White, but he convinced her he was part Black, like her, and she'd been calling him "That tall Black man with the guitar."

Her reasoning confused me.

"How come you call him Black, Aunt Etta? He sure looks White to me."

"Oh, hush now, Trish. He says he's a Black man, so's he <u>is</u> a Black man."

The day of the revival I arrived early. This wasn't in a church, but in a community hall that was over a hundred years old. The building was all built of redwood and the paneling too had a dark red tone. The stage up front was already lit up, and that "Black" man was up there strumming his guitar. Aunt Etta said he was deaf and wouldn't be able to hear me, to talk to her instead. I had rehearsed my music well and was ready whenever Aunt Etta called on me.

The audience arrived and it was very sparse for a revival. Aunt Etta went up on the stage and talked to the guitar man then announced the program. There were two women who looked like they'd just come in off the street and they had a lot of makeup on and sleazy dresses. After a few numbers from the guitar man Aunt Etta asked the women to come up and dance. They giggled and sashayed together as they went up on the stage and did a flag dance I'd never seen before, twirling the red and purple flags on long poles and dancing around to recorded music. They reminded me of hookers doing baton twirling. They giggled when they were done and went and sat down.

I kept waiting for a turn and was tired of sitting. After more than an hour Aunt Etta got up and said loudly, "Trish, you come on up here!"

I walked carefully to where she stood, down in front of the stage holding a microphone.

"This here's my Baby. She's gonna sing for us. This here's Trish, and she jus' lost her husband! Come on up you two girls, get up here and PRAY for her!"

I felt myself blushing about the same time my knees went weak. But I made myself stand there.

Those girls, hiding their mouths but still kind of giggling came up and stood beside us. Aunt Etta raised her right hand over me and started praying. When she was done, I managed to sing a verse of an easy song, not the one I'd prepared, but easier to remember. When I was done, I went and sat down, feeling shaky inside.

My mind kept repeating, "How could she? How could she?" I knew she meant well, but those girls, I didn't know them at all, and I didn't really like them. And me standing up front felt more like shame than grief, and I knew I was done. Done talking to her, done doing her bidding. I could almost hear Eddie talking in my ear, saying, "Honey, you don't have to do that. Don't do that to yourself anymore."

I sat there another fifteen minutes, then got up and walked out.

Strange thing was, she never called me again. Never said, "Sorry, Trish," never asked me for anything. I wondered if she was still paying attention to that guitar man.

I learned from Social Security that I was now the beneficiary of Survival Benefits that more than doubled my income. When I sat reading the official letter I could hear Eddie saying, "With this money, I thee wed." I shook my head and remembered Aunt Etta prophesying, "If you're married to him you'll be better off if anything happens to him."

And later, much later, because we live in the same town, a nurse friend told me that Aunt Etta wasn't doing well. She had nurse care coming into her home to help her every day, but she was still in her home. I liked that she could stay in her own house. The next Christmas I drove by there, wondering if she were still alive. She always decorated her house at Christmas if she was feeling good. She used to have a giant blown up Santa Claus and reindeer pulling a sleigh put up on the low roof over her front porch. This time there was a giant blown up snow man that looked like the giant Michelin Tire man in the movie "Ghost Busters." I was glad to see she was well enough to have Christmas, and she had her Christmas lights up, but I didn't stop. Another six months went by and I drove past her house again. I slowed way down, looking at the cleanliness of the front porch, which was abnormal. Someone had cut down and removed the collard greens bush. She had once given me a cutting from it and I had planted it in my garden, where it flourished. I went home and searched the local obituaries but did not find her name. I asked around and no one could tell me anything. Maybe she'd been put in a care home. I thought of calling all the care homes in the area and decided not to. I figured a mutual friend might eventually mention her. I realized I didn't want to see her, but wanted to know that she was ok.

Now I recounted my memories of her, mingled with memories of my husband. I lived inside of those memories for several days, staying to myself, puttering in the garden, straightening things in the house. I finally felt I had talked with her and with my husband enough, knew I'd made amends with them and let them go.

Six Doors

Six doors in the house slam at once.

Mother slams the one into the bathroom, closing herself in.

Father slams the bedroom door, closing her out.

Susan, 17, slams the door to her room, hoping to shut out the argument she hears every day. Her twin brother, Sean, bangs the back-door screen as he hurries out to jump on his new Honda bike, cherry red. He pulls on the matching helmet, then revs the Honda motor before pulling into the street.

Two more doors of the house slam loudly, as though caught by wind from a window left open. The streetlights flicker on as Sean moves down the road.

Mother opens the bathroom cabinet, straightens small bottles of aspirin, nose drops, Vaseline, an almost empty prescription of Librax, and an old one of Redelin once used to calm her over-active son. She remembers she should have discarded it. She only straightens the shelves, sees nothing she wants for herself. When one chore is done, she goes to another, straightens the towels, scrubs the toilet, even the floor. The place is immaculate, as clean as a hospital room.

Father eases himself into a chair, unfolds the newspaper, flips through the various sections, lifts out the sports and the comics, refolds the remains with difficulty and irritation, thinking of unfolded road maps and confounded straightenings. He drops the unwanted newsprint to the floor, eyeing it once, knowing it will irritate his wife when she sees it; he missed the magazine rack six inches away.

Susan in turn, whips open her closet, flips through clothes for summer and fall season, changes her mind as she unbuttons her blouse. She turns with a slow grin, stares at her open window, removes blouse and bra, pushes her feet out of tennis shoes, peels off her Levi's and stands naked. She fingers her nipples, daring someone to pass by her window.

Sean on his Honda turns toward his friend's house. He urges Rob to go with him, but pulls out of Rob's driveway before his friend retrieves his bike from the garage. Rob, concerned with the look of Sean's eyes, pushes himself to catch up to Sean, knowing the route he usually takes to the beach.

Sean weaves through the traffic south on Beach Boulevard, cutting in front of one man who flips him the bird. He stops for the red light to turn on Westminster. Rob pulls up behind him as Sean signals. The left turn street light turns green.

Sean roars away, the voice of his bike as angry as he, seeing in his mind's eye his sister standing nude by the window, seeing the light of her colonial lamp glowing behind her. He sees his father nodding and reading. He sees his mother cleaning a room. He hears the slamming of doors as he pushes himself forward.

Rob races behind him, see the red light that Sean has ignored. Rob sees the truck turning left, the man at the wheel assuming the biker is slowing.

No squealing of brakes but the thud of cold metal. Something is thrown far to one side of the road. Whatever the object, it lands in an unused gas station, flips up and rests against an outdated gas pump.

Rob slows his bike as he watches his friend. Sean slides on the asphalt, away to the corner opposite the gas station. He rolls to a stop and twists up under a street light. The man in the truck is amazed and shaking. He tries to open his door.

The woman on night shift at the Seven Eleven lifts the receiver and dials nine-eleven.

Rob leans and groans as he looks at his friend. Sean writhes in pain and blood keeps appearing. Rob cannot form any words. He sees that Sean's left leg is gone.

Police sirens.

Red-blue lights flashing, incessant rhythm. Pink tongues of flares laying in columns on the road. Noises rushing, pulsing heavy water sound. People staring from car windows, driving past too slowly. Curious kids crowding and pushing, the boldest one poking close to Sean's misery.

Three policemen using flashlights, frantically search the street for Sean's dismembered portion, poking through broken glass and the crushed metal of Honda. One man yells from the darkened corner of the gas station, his strong stomach revolting as he picks up and cradles Sean's leg, as if it were a child.

Rob is cold, holding Sean's head too tightly in his hands. Policemen work over Sean's body trying to stop blood.

Wind churns as though storm is coming. Dirt and debris fly as cops squint their eyes. Rob watches; Sean's eyes are glazed. A helicopter lands in the darkened unused parking lot behind the gas station. The big wind continues while the blades keep churning.

Susan lies on the bed and writhes with self-wrought pleasure and touching. She hums to her radio, which drones, by her side. Her eyes are wide as she stares at the window, then she turns and gasps as she stares into the lamp bulb.

Sean's father has moved to the living room now; he flips on the television to watch the news hum. Sean's mother is sweeping the white kitchen flooring. She stops to wipe the dirt from the plastic straws of the broom.

The autumn night turns cooler. A gust of wind blows through the kitchen window. One door catches the breeze and slams hard, startling three people alone in their rooms.

David's Wheel

(A fairytale for grown up folk)

There was a stream of water running down the side of a very steep mountain, which seemed to be made of pure silver, the way it shone and glittered in the light of the sun. It never stopped flowing, winter, spring or summer. In the fall the water turned gold under autumn sun and carried the orange-red leaves of autumn trees. Whenever David came to bathe under this waterfall he came alone, and each time he stayed to sit down to rest. He brought with him one day, silver metal to make a ring, and he sat for long hours in the waning sun, making it fine.

It was not a common ring, but one of an odd shape, two V's come together like a small piece of lightning, and in this he put his magic. He placed stars on it, meaning the warmth of the sun. feet of a bird were on it, meaning the steps he had taken carefully to make a good life, and on one side, one side only, there was the form of a tear. He placed it there for his loneliness and placed it on the inside where none could see, keeping it to himself. He put the ring on his finger as he watched the sun go down, glowing red and purple. He sat until darkness came, touching the ring and dreaming, and he never took it off again.

In the forest, there was a woman who sat combing her hair. It was long and dark and drew the lights from the sun and she kept them, tangled tightly in that dark web of hair to keep her warm by night and day. In the night, she sat by a fire, her children deep in sleep and dreaming though never crying. If they dreamed a painful thing and tossed, she soothed their heads and tried to take the pain away. She had left a home with a gold-lined hearth, but with a man of cold heart. She knew she would rather brave storms of raging winter and the open winds of an unsheltered place, than remain in a house with no love.

On her finger she also wore a silver ring to remind her that she still had love locked inside her. On it were etched her many tears as she wished for a home. The tears were visible to anyone who looked at it and the design spun around the whole width of her finger. She put it on and never took it off, believing it held her heart.

David sat long hours spinning dreams and making wishes, keeping them all inside of him and never speaking ill of anything aloud. He only longed for things and never reached for them.

By the stream in the forest, the same that began at the place of the falling water, the woman too had no place for dreams to go, and so she worked, building a home to make safe walls around her children.

In the Spring one year the woman walked alone and came to the falls, early in the morning. The light was so bright and the water so crystalline that her heart sang with joy inside of her. She seldom bathed without her clothes, so modest was she around her children, but this once, in warm spring sunlight, and with joy full in her heart, she took her clothes off and stood under the falling water, feeling very clean and very whole. And the man David came and stood still, startled to find her there. He didn't make a sound, and she did not see him. He watched and something broke inside his heart; something ached inside his chest, and he stood as if frozen and dumb. As she looked up she saw him and became ashamed, ashamed for him to see her. She had not meant for him to see her.

She screamed only once, one loud, long "No!" And then she ran. She ran quickly, deftly, like a mother deer, back to the forest, back to her children, back to where she had left them, and she decided. She decided never to come out of the forest again. Never to stand under the falling stream, never to stand naked in the sunlight. But something had broken inside of her heart too, and her ring burned upon her finger. She could not forget the man's eyes. She could not forget the startled look in them as he stared at her, and she wondered, she kept wondering, how it would feel to wipe the hair from his forehead, and how it would feel to touch his lips with her fingertips. She dreamed of him at night, and in the day when she meant to be working, his face would appear. She would work harder and faster, trying to escape his face.

It was time for David to enter into marriage, and thus he did, taking him to wife the woman chosen for him by his family. His father and mother had taught him wisely and the woman he married was a good woman of the village, adept in teaching the skills of home-making to all young women. She was not homely, but pleasant, and she was good to him, but there remained in him that silent, dreaming hunger. He left off going to the falls, never crossing even the path that led there, and he worked hard in governing the tribe of his people. In the nights, he would lie down by his wife and all would be so quiet. They had two sons and taught them well, teaching them to do good to all people.

But David's dreams betrayed him. No matter how he worked or lived, he dreamed. His mind would not be the proper thing he wanted. In the night the long-haired woman would come to him and stand before him, and tears were in her eyes. He would lift a hand and touch her breast, then she would run silently away. And he would awake, feeling all the tears his loneliness could make, and they no longer would be retained inside the secret circle of his ring.

In the winter of the year, when all the ground was frozen, when leaves were gone from trees and work had stopped in his village, he quietly walked away one day, feeling he must see the stream of silver water just once more. His shoes were warm and his legs wrapped against the cold, but a chill started up through him from the ground and he shivered. He stood at the falls and marveled at the stream that gave off warmth even in the cold of winter, and he thought he saw the woman there, standing in the mist that rose when the water's spray met the cold of the air. But he knew she was gone.

David went back again to his tribe, to his people, and thought he would never again see the woman, and never return to the falling waters. He knew if he went there he would never leave the place, but live and die there if he must, waiting for the woman to return. He knew where he must stay, feeling responsible for his own people, though he knew he could never look at anything again that would seem quite the same as that warm bright day and the feeling he had had when the woman had turned toward him.

The wheel of days came and went, and sometimes they each, the man and woman, would think of each other in their distant places, never without longing, but always without hope. David worked and the woman worked and seemed to be doing good things.

A fire came to the forest and the woman tried to prepare. Long before it reached her, she smelled the smoke and she used her knowledge to protect her children. She dug ditches wide around her home-place, and soaked each of her children's clothing with water. She spread blankets inside the home, preparing and placing food there to be carried away. When the fire drew near and began to rage, animals bounded through the clearing. She gathered her children, gave them warning and teaching, and they ran together through the one narrow channel she could find to safety. She pushed her children carefully through, out of danger of the fire, out of the forest. She followed the stream and it brought her out again, this time with her family, back to the falling waters.

In the ring of safety of the pool of water she waded with her children and wept, then sat on the banks with them. The children laughed at their good fortune and thus could not understand their mother's tears.

"We are blessed," she said, and then imagined the man standing there. She lowered her head to block the vision and still she could feel the look of his eyes. She wanted to run back alone into the flaming forest, knowing loneliness would haunt her.

That same day David felt a very heavy heart and could not stay away. He walked, then ran to reach the pool at the foot of the falling water. And there she sat. He watched her with her head bent down; he watched the children as they sat around her, halos of light on them, each where the sun hit their hair. But the woman's hair was fairest of all to him, yet he could not approach, and she did not lift her head. She only wept and waited, wishing for a hand.

At the foot of the falls, the children rose and danced a circle around their mother as she continued to weep. She did not hear his footsteps coming closer and he did not rush wildly in. He stood for long moments, studying her and thinking what best he could do. He had left behind too much to move now like a wanton lion. The children stopped and looked at him, then laughed again, and ran off into the distance, playing.

He gently, softly, knelt down to her, afraid again she would disappear, the woman of the light and warm long hair. He touched her once, just touching sunlight, and she looked up into his face. She thought she looked into God's face himself, and could not move for wonder. He opened his arms, like eagle wings, and gently, gently, he pulled her to him and encircled her.

Escape

By night he slept beneath a hollowed-out Redwood log in the marshland outside of town. The log was a burl section of wood with the hole enlarged by a fire years before. Clumps of marsh grass grew high around the twisted log, enclosing the entry way. The hole was large enough for a big dog or a thin man to crawl in. once inside the cave-like opening, the hollow was large enough for the man to sit up, move around, and get comfortable. With a portion of a black plastic bag he made a bed that was moisture proof, and he found that laying directly on the earth was comforting, not hard or unyielding. A sheltering place.

Once the man had been quite ample, but now he was thin enough to crawl under and into the log. Neither tall nor short, he had eaten well, lived well by modern standards, and had found himself still wanting. His wife had left him long ago for a 'more passionate' man (though he knew himself that his own dissatisfaction was seated in unfulfilled hidden passion). She had left him completely, with no remnants of their former life and friendship, nothing left for him to anchor any memories.

He had made a good deal of money, worked hard, was respectable. Industrious, reliable – right up till the moment when he walked away. And he had always done things rightly, even giving a two week notice to his boss that he was leaving. He paid off even his utilities, closed all accounts, making sure he left no unpaid debts. He was very thorough.

On his last day of work, he shook hands with colleagues, wished them well, hugged one or two of them, with no rancor against anyone.

As he left his rented home he turned the key in the lock, placed the key in the mailbox, and began walking. On that day he had carried one change of clothes, a warm coat, and money in his pocket, but that had been long ago. He had studied out his actions beforehand, but how he kept going now he did not fathom. Sometimes he knew it was by the kindness of others and sometimes it was by his own wariness and carefulness. He had been many places. First he had travelled northward, near the California Coast, but inland far enough not to feel the ocean cold.

His several small ailments ceased,

except for a nagging pain in his left knee when he travelled any distance. He had had stomach problems, caused by rich and abundant foods that he loved, and by the never ceasing tensions of the work-world he had been a part of. When he had walked long enough, fasted long enough, he found the tastes of things were keen on his tongue, and his stomach no longer hurt. Once without food and not wanting to leave things to chance, he spent two days in a library, studying edible wild foods, memorizing many plants, and taking notes to avoid poisonous plants. He was never without sustenance now, able to choose from natural things, able to survive away from towns and seldom panhandling. He preferred being away from towns and people, especially well-meaning (or otherwise) policemen. He moved northward by sun or moon. Inclement weather always announced itself early, easier now for him to read the signs. Then he would search for shelter and make-do until the storm had passed.

He did not carry much. A comb for his hair, a plastic bag for moisture shield, a few roots to chew on when food did not present itself. He stayed away from large towns and people unless his shoes and feet gave out. This one thing for his feet he did not do Without. Panhandling could yield enough to find a thrift store with sturdy shoes.

In the shelter he had found in the log he was often awakened by the sounds of joggers' foot thuds just before dawn.

He was once startled awake by the snuffling of a large dog who had sniffed him out. Early on this morning he climbed from his place before dawn and before any intruders could bother him. He found himself longing for the sight of the sea. He had been living in the land of the Redwoods for some time. Winter had arrived and descended in the forest with its long rains at the same time he had found his wooded shelter. But this day he longed to smell the salt of the sea and its deep green waters. He walked briskly on the animal pathways along a river. His eyes and ears were acute from long study of nature and wariness of danger, but his desire for the ocean eased his natural state of attention as he walked with determination westward.

He came to a wide highway running north and south and waited there for heavy traffic to pass. He marveled at the sleekness and flashiness of metal and speed as they passed. People looked like parts of machines behind the steering wheels. He stood there realizing how long he'd been away from people and things.

As he was about to set his feet onto the roadway pavement, an older car approached, black, rusted, nameless and dented. It slowed to a stop as it came abreast of him. The young woman driving was red-haired, aquiline nosed, and pouty. The young olive skinned man in the passenger seat grinned at him as the window rolled down. Black haired and thin, the young man leaned out the window asking, "Wanna lift?" the old man's hand flew up to his thin and greying beard. The young man had fierce, bright, green eyes.

The old man's hand raised in a moment to decline the offer, but his mouth said, "Yes." His curiosity and too long aloneness overcame him. The young man reach back and opened the rear door which creaked loudly. The old man seated himself carefully on the worn upholstered seat. He wondered aloud where they were headed.

"You going North?" asked the young man.

"We're only going to Trinidad," said the young woman loudly, as if the old man couldn't hear.

"Oh," replied the old man, realizing he

was out of practice talking to people. He fell silent, nothing else to say, not wanting to ask questions or be aggressive or intrusive.

The highway rose in gradual incline, turned a corner and began to descend. As they rounded the hills they came in full view of the ocean. The shining sun glinted off the cold greenness of ocean, and white caps rolled to the shore on that perfect crescent shoreline. The old man leaned toward the window to stare at the waters. A feeling of coming home rose up in him and he whispered, 'Magnificent!'

The young man turned in the front seat and stared hard at the old man. He didn't speak but his gaze seemed to bore through the old man's skin.

They took a turn off to the right, then to

the left. The old man wondered if he were in danger, not knowing these two.

"You wanna eat with us?" said the young man curtly.

"I have no money," the old man answered.

"That's not what I asked," said the young man.

"We've got food in the back," said the girl.

"Okay," said the old one, weighing and guessing at the personalities and relationship of these two.

The road curved steeply downward and out to a sandy parking lot. A fancy restaurant built half on a pier and half onto the rocky hillside was to the left. An old deteriorating fishing boat sat atop a hillock by the parking lot. A rocky promontory was at center and the roaring ocean tore away from the shore to the right.

The two young people hopped out and went to open the trunk. The old man sat still in the back seat, looking over his shoulder through the crack in the raised lid of the trunk, making sure there was only food in there, nothing dangerous.

The quarrelsome voices of the young man and woman rose behind the raised trunk. They argued about how to fix the simple food they brought out. The old man blinked, memories rising rapidly of his marriage, of the harshness of words, of the uselessness of his caring.

The young woman came back to the front seat with her arms full. She turned to him and smiled sweetly, almost seductively, and he blinked again. She poured some apple juice into a Styrofoam cup for him as the young man sat down in the front seat and slammed the door hard, and began opening a bag of chips.

"Sorry 'bout the door," he said, unusually polite. "It doesn't close easy."

The old man savored the taste of apple juice as the young people put sandwiches together. They layered meat, cheese, lettuce and sauces. He had forgotten how those things tasted. "Thanks," he said and chewed hungrily into wheat bread and commercial foods.

"Where are you headed?" asked the young woman. She wiped mayonnaise slowly from her mouth with the back of her hand. Her fingernails were broken and dirty.

"Right here, this place," said the old man. Then while he chewed he watched her beautiful pale profile and a leafy twig caught in the tangle of her red hair. He imagined the dread locks full of tiny roses and wild flowers.

Then he watched the young man, whose nose was just as hawk-like as the young woman's. His dark skin and prominent cheekbones suggested his ethnicity. The old man said matter-of-factly, "You're Indian."

"Sure," said the young man, his mouth twisting in a smirk. He turned and looked at the old man again with his green eyes, as intense as a hunted animal's.

They finished eating in silence.

The old man reached for the door knob. "I want to walk now. Thanks for the food and the ride." He stood, stretched himself, and knew they weren't done with him yet. He began walking away. He stood atop a huge dune with a steep pathway leading down to the water. The crescent shaped beach was wide and the tide appeared to be very low. Other old cars parked there had surf boards tied to the roof tops and young people looking out toward the horizon, scanning the waves.

The old man stepped and slid down the sandy embankment, noticing the ice plants with delicate yellow blossoms. Sandpipers scuttled away from him as he walked toward the waves. He saw and picked up an orange translucent stone. It was an agate. He rubbed it in his palms and slid it into his pocket. Walking quickly, he noticed that in his preoccupation with the orange stone he could not hear the waves crashing, until he turned and looked toward the ocean. One lone surfer in a black wet suit paddled way out past the breakers, waiting for the tide to turn. The sun was beginning to set off the end of the massive stone hill to the left.

He did not look back toward the parking lot until he was far down the beach and near some huge stone outcroppings. He leaned against the stone and looked back, hoping to be unseen. He could see the black car still sitting there, it's nose just visible at the top of the dune.

The sand beneath his feet felt wonderful. The air and the light made it easier to breathe. He sat down in the sand in the rounded crevice of a rock. He picked up a black feather, noting it was crow or raven, and poked it upright into a mound of sand and said a silent prayer for safety and direction. It was warm in the crevice out of the wind. The waves were a long way out from him. He listened to a gull cry and dozed as the sun set.

He dreamed he was floating atop the waves, undulating, feeling easy. He dreamed as he sat erect with his back against the stone.

"Hey Dude!" said the young man.

The old man started awake, looking straight into the young man's green eyes who squatted in front of him.

"We were wondering if you were okay."

The old man looked up to see the young woman standing behind the young man, one hand on her hip. She was grinning, as if she had what she wanted.

"Sure. I'm okay." The old man stood up slowly, stiff in the knees. He watched the sand drop off him and bent to empty the cuffs of his pants.

"You want to stay the night with us?" the young man asked. "We have a camper just north of here. You can sleep warm and dry tonight. There's plenty of room."

The old man shrugged, thinking they had found him and would follow him until they were done with him. He considered feigning that he had a place to go, but that might not put them off.

He dusted the sand from his pantlegs again without answering, then followed the young man back up the dunes. The young woman lagged behind the old man but he felt coldness come into his kidneys and turned around often to see where she was.

They drove the beat up black car northward in near darkness and pulled into a side road among tall trees. Their camper was set among high bushes, decidedly old but still intact. The old man wondered where the truck was that had brought the camper here, but didn't ask. He noted that it was leveled perfectly. The young man unlocked the door. As the old man climbed in he saw that in every bit of wall space there were paintings, exquisitely painted: small scenes, some of cafes, some of beaches, and one of a beautiful curly haired child.

"Whose are these?" asked the old man.

"Mine," said the young man. "I'm an artist." The young man's voice remained hard. There was a table with a padded bench, then a full bed where the camper fit over a truck cab. Everything was grimy grey-brown, except the paintings, that stood out like jewels.

"These are very good." Said the old man. He reached up and tapped the edge of one for emphasis.

"I know," said the young man, then pulled himself up to the high bed and hunched down, it being too short for him to sit up straight. He stared down at the old man. The lights were dim as the young man habitually pulled out a tobacco pouch and rolled a cigarette. The match struck and lit up the small paintings reflecting the brief light.

"You sell them?"

"Sometimes," The young man said.

"Not enough." Said the young woman with sarcasm in her voice. "You sleep over there," She said to the old man and pointed to the bench beside the table. She began unbuttoning her blouse, revealing her small breasts in the dim light.

The old man looked away from her, found a blanket beside the bench and prepared for sleep. His natural weariness overcame him then and he rested.

Toward morning he turned and could smell the odor of musty roses. It was still too dark to see but he could feel the warmth of another body close at hand. He could feel eyes watching him. It made him think of a cat's eyes, the way a cat would stare long, waiting for a mouse or other prey to move. He lifted an arm. His hand brushed against a long tress of hair just above him. He felt a thin hand grab his arm tightly. A body, warm and eager pressed against him, bare breasts pushed against his face. His throat itched. He did not cry out. He coughed, then coughed again. A mighty spasm rose up in his throat. The thin hand pressed his mouth momentarily to silence him, but flew off as the cough increased. He sat straight up, his throat barking loudly. He reached across to where he thought the door should be, still coughing, nearly falling out of the camper as the door gave way from the weight of his body.

He caught himself on the door frame, turned his back to the doorway and eased down slowly. He walked backward a few steps, looking at the door of the camper and up into a starlit morning. A thin pale arm, a bare shoulder and breast showing faintly in the starlight looked ghostly as the arm reached out silently for the door knob and pulled the camper door shut.

The old man cleared his throat several times, spitting into the bushes. He turned around and walked cautiously on the dirt roadway till he reached the empty night highway. He crossed the road and entered the forest again, slowly picking his way until he found a path made by silent animals, and continued walking slowly, deliberately, making the distance wider between himself and the camper, until he knew he was alone.

Coyote Man and Turquoise Woman

"Hey, Coyote Man!" The woman called out the slightly open window as she saw Coyote running alongside her car. She wanted to know which direction he was headed so she could avoid him. She was very much afraid that he would change the color of his graying coat and the look of his too-orange eyes by the time she crossed paths with him again.

"What d'ya have in your satchel, Coyote?" She kept the car at a slow pace.

"Stop calling me that name!" he growled in irritation.

The woman laughed at him good-naturedly with a wide smile. She had gaps between her once beautiful and perfect teeth, gaps put there by Coyote Man himself. She had been his favorite sport these past many years until she quit putting up with his game. "Castling heart and hand" he'd called it, from his knowing how to play chess so well. She called him a cheat and liar but it did no good. His motto had been a combination of things like, "love 'em, leave 'em, make 'em cry, and call 'em all bitches before you die." He'd strung this line out so far and so long that it became a dirge, worse than chalk on slate, more raucous than crows' cries. He had sung his complaining heart out to this Turquoise Woman loud and long.

"You got something in that little valise you can't tell me about?" She asked. Her interest was genuine.

"None of your damn business," he replied, as if he'd planned on saying this to her for quite some time.

She called out, her lips puckered a little, "Kiss me again, won't you Coyote Man?" and when he responded with a sneer she stuck her tongue out at him—just a little—and ever so affectionately. He stopped trotting, his feet hurt so much, he stopped altogether, very tuckered out and foot sore. He lifted his right foot up and balanced himself adroitly, picking at the sore spot in the middle of his foot.

She watched him then from the rear-view mirror, pulling ahead of him, but carefully keeping him in sight. He was dangerous alright. More dangerous if you looked too long in the kind façade of his glowing eyes. Why, right now she suspected he could bend down and pick up a stone and put it through her window before she could brace herself. Better yet, he'd aim for the sun roof opening and cause it to hit her on the head, knock her lights out, twist her brain, render her unconscious one more time. Yeah, it could happen. It had happened. Best keep him with his shaggy coat just in view, don't be in too big a hurry to let him off the hook, since she was sure he was cooking up a new batch of rotten eggs to let fly at her.

She stopped the car but reached over to make sure the door was locked. She rolled the window down far enough to yell at him, but not enough for him to get his hand all the way into the car.

"Hey, Coyote Man! You want a ride?" He came right up to the window, pressed his dog-like lips on it. "Say that again, Bitch." He snarled, pulled a weird face, then made an obscene gesture at her.

She laughed again. "Is that all you've got to say for yourself, Man?" she began to unbutton her blouse seductively. "Is that all, after all these years?" Don't you want a ride, Man?" She defined the words by licking her lips slowly, remembering his favorite porno magazines, figured she'd do things the way he liked, make him sweat a little. She tugged at the hem of her skirt slightly, as if she might raise it a little higher.

"Now what are you going to do out there, Coyote Man, out there in the desert all alone? Oh, yeah, you have companions, that Big Dog of a man, and that scruff of a new woman, but what are you going to <u>do</u> out there with no challenges to your Manhood? What are you gonna do when you want someone to soothe your hot-headed, hard-hearted, hooded eyes kind-of-face? You know, someone who <u>knows</u> you, Man. What are you gonna do?"

"You want to come back home now, Turquoise Woman? I'll sweep up around the fire pit and put Dog Man out to dry. You could come home now."

"Home?" Her voice broke a tiny shell's worth. She spit a little through the gap in her teeth, like she was spitting out that tiny shell that made her feel some pain. "Home," she repeated, made it sound like a pillow, a lost pillow. She leaned down to look him better in the eye.

"Man," she continued more strongly. "You've got to be kidding, I don't believe in polygamy. Leave that to the Mormons. And even if you get rid of that frowsy little dame I saw you leaning into the other day, even if you sent her off, there's not enough room left over by your fire pit for me when you get done dancing around there with your fancy mind, your fancy plans, your big gray tail, your toothy grin, your swelled-up tummy full of all the good things I put there. There's no room for me there. No siree! This Turquoise Woman's got a lot of work to do and too much fun to have while I'm at it. You just press your lips up here again so I can rev up my motor."

Coyote Man couldn't believe his eyes. She had a new look to her. She had been so gentle, docile, so giving. He didn't know now what to expect of her. She turned the ignition key, started up the car, and slowly took her foot off the brake. She kept him still in her peripheral vision, noticing that somehow his lips had not moved from the smooth glass surface of the window. He seemed stuck there like a large suction cup, and now she could not believe <u>her</u> eyes.

She turned now to watch him, astounded at this vision. He hooked his fingers in through the open window, gripping for a good hold. He was hunched over. Surely his feet must be up on the running board as the car was moving forward ever more swiftly, she not looking forward, so fascinated with him hanging on her window. She could see distinctly the slightly red veins in his canine gums and the pink flesh as he tried to wiggle his lips free. His tongue, all moist fleshy muscle strained in his distress and pushed against the glass like a starfish stomach.

Now Turquoise Woman made herself turn and look at the road. She had not veered to right or left and looked down the straight black highway, wondering just how far this road went in such a beautiful straight line. She pressed her foot down gently. She was always careful in everything she did. She kept on pushing. She watched the speedometer needle climb slowly. At thirty miles an hour, she looked over to see how he was doing. Just fine, she thought. At fifty miles, she leaned and smiled at him. "How am I driving?" She called sweetly. At sixty-five miles per she noticed the whites of his eyes were showing. She called, "I knew you liked the thrill of the road." She settled in like a long-distance driver and after about an hour of this nice, gleaming, unbending road, she glanced from speedometer to dog-tired, pop-eyed Coyote Man. "Say, did you know this car can do 90 miles without a shimmy?" The whites of his eyeballs rolled up like a slot machine and filled the cavern where his irises should have been. The black skin of his lips was lacerated at the edges, but still stayed in place on that window. The tongue had grown slack, as had his body, except his hands which still seemed to grasp the window. His body seemed to have deflated, his furry carcass had become a flag, his legs now flapping out in the breeze, the clawed feet rattling like old bones in the wind.

Turquoise Woman sighed and slowed down to the speed limit.

"Hey, Coyote Man," she said softly. She looked over at him with tenderness, and a lot of tiredness. "Didn't I warn you? I told you not to mess with me anymore. You didn't quite know what I meant, did you?" She clicked her tongue, said one more word, "Sorry," and kept on driving.

Part II

Amerige

Amerige
A Parable of Children

There once was a land called Fair Haven where all the children lived in joy and peace. They could work and play without fear of harm, for in this place their mothers and fathers had established a land of justice and mercy.

In Fair Haven a girl-child grew whose name was Amerige. She was much like the other children of the land, for she had lived without fear. Thus she thought that people everywhere were kind and gentle, like the people of Fair Haven.

Amerige was beautiful, with fair skin and hair of red-gold color. Her hair was long, and when she danced, which was often, her hair swung out behind her, catching light and throwing off a beautiful glow. She laughed and played daily with her friends, and yet she was good to her parents, careful to work with them also. She was very wise for a child of only seven.

On a warm summer day a boy came to Fair Haven, walking barefoot and alone. He had come from a place called Dark City, looking for a new home. He was dirty and his clothes were ragged, but when Amerige saw him, she did not mind the dirtiness of his skin, nor the condition of his clothes. She took his hand and welcomed him.

"What is your name?" She asked. "Mine is Amerige. Say it, Ah-mer-eej."

"Ah-mer-eej?" He faltered, copying her.

"What's yours?" She persisted.

"My name?" I have no name," he said, "Not like yours...no, I have no name."

She pressed him with questions, which he refused to answer, telling her only that he came from Dark City. "It's a land of sorrow, of heavy burdens," he said. "I came here to look for peace."

They walked together and laughed at times, and she showed him all the lovely places she knew, and all of it was home to her.

She could not know, she could not see, that the boy's face was badly bruised beneath the dirt that covered his skin. She could not know of the places he had been, but she danced for him and he smiled. His eyes held some dark and secret pain, which Amerige, for all her young wisdom, could only imagine. She did not have the heart to ask him to tell her.

All day long they played. She showed him a fountain in the center of town, and she danced circles around him until he grew dizzy from watching her. As the day grew on her friends came around and tried to talk to the new boy and to include him in their games.

Her friend Enrique, whose day of birth was the same as hers, and whose hair was as dark as Amerige's was light, carried a golden ball. He tried to show the new boy how to play. Amerige stood by, puzzled by the Dark City boy, for he pulled back, seemed to shrink within himself.

Still Enrique called out to him, "Please, come and play. It is such an easy game."

Thus Enrique pressed the boy, even as Amerige had done. He pushed the golden ball into the Dark City child's two hands. The boy grew angry. Amerige ran to his side.

"What's wrong?" She asked, but it was too late. The boy's anger came out of fear, and he hit Enrique as hard as he could, dropping the golden ball and crying all at the same time. Amerige tried to stop him, but he shoved her once with all his might, then he pushed her hard again, this time making her fall.

Her hand was cut and bleeding, and her knees were bruised, but as the Dark City boy ran away she ran after him, calling and calling.

"Please come back!" She called. "Tell me what is wrong!"

But he kept on running, until he disappeared completely from her view.

The sun was setting as he ran from town, and when Amerige finally gave up hoping for his return she walked home. She cried as she thought of him. She knew he would be in the dark of night alone, while she was able to go home.

She told her mother and father about the boy, and no matter what they said to her, the tears continued. She could not understand why he had been so angry, why he had hit Enrique, or why he had knocked her down.

"You do not know, Amerige, where the boy came from," said her father, trying to calm her with reason's voice.

"And you cannot know what the world is

like," said her mother as she grieved with her, "Outside of this place we have called Fair Haven."

"The boy was hurting on the inside," said her father.

"Is that why then," questioned Amerige, "He had to hurt me too?"

"Some people," her mother said, almost whispering, "When they are hurt too long, or very deeply, allow their hearts to turn to stone."

"He was not like that," insisted Amerige. "He was kind to me till the other children came."

Then both the mother and father put their arms around their cherished daughter, but her weeping did not cease.

From that day on Amerige was changed. No matter how glad she felt and no matter how she grew, though she smiled and danced, she did not forget the boy from the Dark City. Where she had fallen and cut her hand, a small scar remained on her palm to remind her of him. Thus, she learned that joy and peace are rare, and she knew she must show her own joy and sorrow in her dance. And she knew a time would come when she would give back love and caring to the world of the Dark City.

Part II

Removing the Masks of Self

Kim's Treasures

St. Croix, USVI

Gallows Bay

I thought I had come to the islands for Cruzan stories, of the survivors of the slaves brought to the Danish colonies. I roomed in a hotel for a while but it was too expensive. As I was looking for a place to live I met a Vietnamese woman who had had a restaurant until a hurricane 3 years before had damaged her property extensively and she had not been able to restore the premises. She had five apartments above the restaurant, which were still intact, and she invited me to room there.

I had planned to stay on the island for one month, but after three weeks, the airlines went on strike and I was forced to stay. I felt stranded with no way off the island. "You'll be okay with me," said Kim. "You are like a refugee on this Island," she said. "I have been refugee too. You stay with me." She showed me the upstairs rooms where three of them had been restored. We each had a private room and in one room with a kitchenette we cooked and shared our meals.

She gave me free rein of the place and I explored the upstairs a little when she was working downstairs in what was left of the restaurant. I looked in the rooms we could not use and found the remnants of broken furniture left from the hurricane all piled up in a haphazard manner. As I was poking around, looking at Asian paintings with broken frames, I uncovered a small jade Buddha, the size of my hand. It was one of the chubby smiling Buddhas and I saw that it had a large crack in it, but it was still in one piece. I was intrigued with the little statue and reasoned in myself that Kim was now a Catholic, maybe she had been all her life, and from the way it had been discarded, she didn't need the statue or consider it of value. I carried it back to my room and tucked it in between my clothing, still in my suitcase.

Over our shared meals Kim Ng began telling me her life stories, pieces at a time.

This is how the story unfolded. In Saigon her family owned a large acreage with six hundred coconut palms. A beautiful place, very serene, very safe, she said. The family would go for picnics out under the trees. There were six brothers and sisters; Kim was the youngest. One sister was born the same year that I was and one brother, born in the year of the Tiger, was older than me. That brother was very aggressive and Kim said, "It is not good for a girl to be born the year of Tiger. She get in trouble, too aggressive!"

During the few weeks that I lived with Kim, she took me to church every Sunday. The windows of the chapels had no screens or glass, but large wooden shutters that were open and pushed back against the walls. No glass because they would be too easily broken during strong storms and hurricanes. When the breeze blew it was refreshing in the tropical heat. I enjoyed sitting in the diverse congregation with her, people from many places and of every complexion.

Kim wanted to show me how to navigate around the island. She had a car and I had already had the experience of riding the bus with long walks between where I was left off and where I needed to go. I was grateful for her transporting me. I had been on the bus one day and pulled the buzzer cord to tell the driver I wanted to get off. Five Black women's faces all turned to me and said at once, "Not now. This is not right!" It was closer to my destination, but not a regular stop.

Kim took me with her to do all her business. She had been an Asian Beauty with beautiful skin, a sparkling smile, and a certain way of moving her hips to make her more attractive. Now she was in her 50's and still she moved like a lithe young woman. In one shop she approached the counter where the man greeted her in a serious manner and when she turned on her charm, giving him her sweetest smile, his face did not change and his voice was flat, no enthusiasm. He turned his back on her and I watched her change her demeanor to match the situation. Her girlishness left, and in its stead was a small but very strong woman of quiet determination.

Back home she began teaching me how to make a Vietnamese dish with soup and meatballs. "You can tell the meat is done," she said, "when the meatballs rise and float in the soup." Then she began telling me about her home in Viet Nam.

Kim's father was mayor in Saigon, she said. "Very smart, very respected. He knew martial arts, very strong and able to defend his family if needed. But when the communists came in they watched him all the time."

"Finally they came and took him late one night, tied him up," Kim said. "He didn't fight. They told him they were taking him to a meeting. He wanted peace, so he did not fight. He could have gotten away, but he wanted to talk and listen in that meeting."

"The communist soldiers took him to the river. We have two rivers there," Kim said.

"They beat him up bad, then they threw him in the river, still tied up. They thought he would die. Somehow he freed himself from the ropes and he swam back to shore. Then they killed him. We never saw him again."

"After that, my mother got very sick, very fast. She die."

"Now I do not go back to Viet Nam for a long time. It hurts too much. The government – they took our land. The chemicals from bombs, Napalm - they kill all the trees. Sometime my one sister, she tries to get some of the land back. She got an attorney, showed her papers, but the government does not give back anything. Now their office building sits on our land. One time I go there with her; she has me help her, but the government doesn't give any answer. It makes me feel very bad."

"I was youngest of six children. Very spoiled. Everyone thinks I will be no good. My father still carried me around in his arms when I am 7 or 8. I loved him very much. When I go to high school – I don't like it. I don't want to go. Mama and Daddy say, "Don't make her go!" Every day I get up I tell my Mama I'm sick. My stomach hurts. She not make me go. Later, I want to go to cooking school to learn Chinese cooking, and to sewing school. My dad says, "You let her go. That other school not good for her anyway. She wants to cook and sew."

"So that's what I did. Later, after I marry my husband, we move and I go to cooking school in Paris. I get fat! 138 pounds! I have to taste every day, four years. Wow!"

"In Viet Nam, my family work very hard. We have small store. Army men come there every day. One man, a Lieutenant, asked me if I want to work for him in his office. I'm smart so he sends me to learn typing. He is old, like my father. He wants me to be his daughter. His wife lives and waits for him in Korea. They want to adopt me, take me over there. He writes to her, sends her pictures of me. His wife sends me clothes, presents, all the time. They ask my family, "Can they adopt me?" I said, "I like you, but I must stay here with my family." Later, he transfers. Then my future husband comes into the office. He's also a Lieutenant, but young. I work for him.

He comes to meet my family. He shops in our store. Everybody likes him. He's very nice. He's good to everybody. We be friends. We go to the show. He comes to my home for dinner. After seven months he asks me to marry him. I say, "What?" I'm shocked. I say – "You let me think for one month. You leave me alone, let me think." So that's what happens. He comes back later and says, "What happened?" I say, "I think you will leave me some time. Divorce me. You leave me over there – in Europe or America, and I have nobody. My family is all here."

" "I will not leave you," my husband says. "I mean this forever." So I say okay."

"I go to find my older brother in a refugee camp. This is about 1977-78. My husband, our home, is in France. I go to Singapore. I'm sitting there every day for a month. Fifty dollars a day, very expensive. I have papers to get into the refugee camp where my brother lives. Very dangerous."

"My husband is in the army. He gets me papers to travel, but now in Singapore the American Embassy says too dangerous. Government will not let you enter. My brother is somewhere in Indonesia. You go in – you can get in, but you no come out. That's what they tell me."

"So I call my husband. He was then in Belgium. He does not want me to go in, but I say, "I've been here one month. It's very expensive. I came all this way to see my brother, to find out where he wants to go, USA or Europe. I have to find him!" My husband says he's scared for me, but I say I'll be okay."

"So I get ready, have all these papers, a letter from the UN, a U.S. citizen paper, and passport. I must leave everything in the U.S. Embassy except passport. That way, if anything happens to me, I say to the authorities that the U.S. Embassy in Singapore has all my papers. They know I'm here."

"I get on a boat, they tell me I must go past two islands. This is a hospital ship. They pick up sick people from the refugee camp, doctor them for a week or so, then bring them back to the camp when well. They say to me, "You can't go to the camp! You're crazy!" At that time no family members could visit refugees. It did not happen before me. Only people getting in are Red Cross, Catholics, and doctors. Nobody else."

"I met Father Mike, an American Priest, in Viet Nam. He lives there thirty years. He knows the Viet Nam North dialect and the South dialect, many ways, better than me. He laughs at me, says I speak like a foreigner. He's White but sounds like a Vietnamese."

"We go past islands. We get to the place where camps are. Two women on the boat who were sick are being returned to the camp after their hospital stay. One woman says, "Who are you? You're not a refugee." I say, "No, I'm American now. I come to look for my brother."

"Who is he?" She asks. I tell her his name and how he looks. She says, "I know him. He lives in the camp site next to mine." So this is how I find my brother."

"The soldiers take me to the refugee camp. I meet the commander. He likes me. I tell him about my brother. I have to go inside this fence. I stand there on cement all day. The heat has been 110-115 degrees all this time. I have nothing to eat or drink. The guard says to me, "You hungry?" and I say, "Oh yes." He brings me tea, and those small bananas, very sweet. "You want more?" He asks. "I say yes. Then I have a whole bunch of the sweet bananas."

"My brother – back then if the guard comes to get a person who lives in the camp, they give no explanation. If your name is called you may get beaten, or disappear forever. So when the guards called my brother, he is very upset. His wife and 5 year old son cry very much. They are all very frightened."

"So I was there waiting all day. Finally – I see them bringing my brother in a jeep. I am inside the fence. We have not seen each other for many years, but he recognizes me. He jumps out of the jeep while it is still going and runs to get me. We are very excited. He is crying."

"Then that night the soldiers bring his wife and son to stay with us. The commander comes to talk to me. He shares his tent with us, puts a canvas partition as a wall down the middle of the tent. He let us stay together there. This is very nice, but every night, my nephew, the 5-year-old, he pee very bad in the night all over the floor. The floor is covered with straw mats for rugs, but the smell stays in there. I can't sleep."

"Next day the commander sees me. I look sick, kind of green. He says, "Oh Kim, you no look good. What's wrong?" So I tell him. No good sleeping like that. Too hot and there is the smell of pee. I can't rest. So he orders the tent to be opened up. They wash out the whole thing. He gives me his bed to sleep in and goes to sleep somewhere else."

"Later he tells me, "Kim, I really like you. You're so nice and I'm divorced. I'd like you to be mine." I tell him thank you. He's very kind to help me. I so appreciate him watching out for me, but I have a husband already. I'm sorry about the commander. But he is good to my brother from then on, and each time I write to my brother, I send the commander a post card from a different place in the world and tell him thank you again. So you see how this works."

"Six months later my brother and his family are sent to Paris. We meet him there. I find him a job and his wife a job. I take care of them in my home, feed and clothe them. I tell them "Save all your money for one year, then you go out on your own, so they do that."

"But my sister-in-law starts getting mean to me. She says, "You open a restaurant for me. I will be the cook." I say, "No, you don't speak English yet. First you learn, so you can talk to customers, then I open one for you." She says no. She's very greedy. Later, after they move out, she's so mean to my brother that they split up."

Later Kim tells me that there in her St. Croix home, she has a few palm trees. Each year she has lived there her husband buys her a young palm tree and she nurtures it, along with the ones from years before, remembering their beautiful Coconut Palm Grove in Viet Nam. Her husband lives in Europe, where his work is headquartered and she lives in St. Croix.

She invites me to dinner with her Vietnamese friends who live on the island. I realize this evening that sitting amongst them that I am at ease. I feel like one of their relatives, not a stranger. Then one of them asks Kim, "You have any Buddha statues? Maybe we can set up an altar here." She says, "I had a small jade one, but I can't find it. It went through the hurricane and I put it with all the broken things. It no longer seems to be there." My face flushes red but I cannot make myself speak up. I had intended to take it home with me to the states and I am too embarrassed to admit that I have it in my room.

And that is the way it ends. The airplane workers end their strike and I can go home. I fly home to the States, unpack my clothes and set that little green Buddha on a prominent shelf where I am reminded of Kim almost daily. I learn and repeat the Buddhist saying often, "Do not take anything that is not offered."

Lowered Faces

(A story of Refugee Women in the 1970s)

I answer the phone with a honeyed voice saying, "Doctor's office, may I help you?" I handle all the front office business, and then if the doctor needs help I take the phone off the hook and go into the back office. He's an obstetrician and just opening his own office after his hospital residency, which means he takes any cases coming his way. Our welfare cases are often Vietnamese Boat People who need care.

A woman named Mrs. Baxter leads a very tiny Vietnamese woman in whose belly is swollen with child and concealed under thick clothing.

Mrs. Baxter reminds me of lean-looking missionaries of the Baptist Church, ones sent to Africa and Asia. She is tall and bony and has an unkempt look about her. Mrs. B carries her own baby with her balanced on her hip. She and her husband are the sponsors of the

Vietnamese woman's family. Mrs. B's dark hair loops in large, uncontrolled curls around her pallid, narrow face.

Mrs. Baxter launches into talk with missionary zeal about Sing Da's diet, living habits, and scantily known medical history. I try to catch it all, but the woman's voice irritates me and I try to shut her out of my mind.

I turn to Sing Da and am startled at the intelligence and fear in her small, moon-shaped face. I touch her arm reassuringly and she follows me to an exam room. She is learning English and I say carefully, "How are you?"

"I yam fine," she repeats dutifully. She smiles shyly, then looks down at the floor. We seem to be nodding at each other and I suddenly feel Asian, bowing and nodding.

It is summer, but Sing Da wears her clothing in many layers, with a dirty yellow padded nylon jacket on top of it all. Everything is brightly colored, mismatched like Salvation Army cast-offs.

In the bathroom I try to explain, gesticulating, that we need a urine sample. She's embarrassed and giggles behind her hand, but understands.

It's time for the doctor to examine Sing Da, but she won't take anything off. I shut the door to the exam room, leaving the doctor standing in the hallway, and show her what I need for her to do. None of us has language to deal with her. The doctor comes into the room, becomes frustrated with her and goes back into the hall, angry.

"Would you please get an interpreter here next time, Mrs. Baxter," he says impatiently.

"Yes, Doctor, but it's hard. She speaks only Hmong dialect, not Vietnamese, and her husband is working." Mrs. Baxter comes into the room with us and explains to me that it's a custom in Viet Nam not to school the women. Mrs. B shifts her plump, pale baby on her hip to her other side when it begins to cry. The baby smells of soured milk and urine soaked clothes. She continues telling me that Sing Da is from the hills, never left them until the war; she had learned her village speech, nothing more. Boys are taught the national language in school. She has birthed four children by herself, perhaps without midwife, surely without doctor or clinic.

Mrs. Baxter goes out to the waiting room and finally Sing Da is ready for exam, taking off only the bottom portion of clothing and clutching the paper sheet over her naked body.

I stand by her side as the doctor examines her. Her eyes are filled with fear and shame. She clutches my hand and we both lower our eyes, embarrassed, ashamed by our womanhood.

Her time arrives. The doctor hurries from the office to the hospital, only a block away. When he returns he unfolds her story to me, as though he is proud to have been a part of it. I imagine Sing Da's round frightened eyes, like a gentle, cornered rabbit, looking for escape.

The doctor smiles at me, standing by the counter at the reception desk, toying with a stethoscope and shifting his weight from foot to foot.

I have cancelled the rest of the patients for the day, Sing Da's birthing stopping the day's routine. I watch the doctor, the smile that touches his mouth, as I lean on the daily posting sheets on my desk, wondering whether he understands the story he tells me.

In the labor room he tells me that Sing Da was fine, the nurses walking around her, timing, checking, patting her arms. When her pains came hard they put her on a gurney to roll her to the delivery room. Half way down the hall she jumped off the moving table and ran back to her labor room, fear preceding everything.

The doctor followed, dressed in his surgical green clothing and mask. He found her in the farthest corner of the room, squatting in a pool of bloody water, her hospital gown hanging loose across her knees, red rivulets running across the polished floor. He did not approach her; her eyes were wild and he could see what she meant to do. She pushed two times and caught the baby, wiped bloody tissue from the baby's face, cleaned the baby's mouth and nostrils with her too-thin brown fingers, and pressed breath gently into the new body with her lips. Then she pulled placenta from herself excellently, with her feet, balancing, cradling the baby close to her in one arm. She looked at the doctor, then turned her face away from him.

I'm sitting at home on a high old stool held together by wire at the bottom. The checks and bills are on the counter in front of me. I am playing cards with checks, shuffling to see which ones not to pay so I can buy some groceries.

This morning the doctor equated me with the pay he gives me and I am still angry about it. I was standing there lining up files on the counter, organizing in my mind how I would get the insurance forms sent off before patients arrived.

"Should we hire an assistant?" He smiled a disarming rugged smile at me, fingering the stethoscope in his lab coat pocket.

"Sure could use one," I said. "There's just too much for me to do as one person."

"Did you check the incubator this morning?" He asked.

I said "No," while he walked into the small lab room and opened the wooden case where we grow specimens.

"Damn," he said, "The temperature's been up. Even the petrie dish melted." He pulled out a warped piece of plastic with dry, cracked brown agar on it. I smiled at the misshapened dish, felt like I should apologize, but I didn't set the temperature and hadn't done anything.

Then, during the afternoon, a young woman came in with an abscess, just four days after childbirth, and the doctor sent her directly over to the hospital with her husband. The young couple was so concerned and she was in so much pain that I took the baby from them and told the young man to come back after he had admitted his wife.

The doctor stopped on his way out for lunch, leaned far over the counter and winked at me as I rocked the new baby against me with one arm and wrote in the appointment book with my free hand.

"You know," he said, "You work really hard, but I think I'm generous in my pay to you."

I looked at him and tilted my head just a little.

"I mean," he continued, "I think you're worth what I pay you, or you seem to earn what I pay."

"Yes," I said, feeling my face redden. "I certainly earn what you pay." The baby began to fuss and I put it to my shoulder, giving it my full attention.

"You'd learn," he said to me with another knowing wink, "If you were in the army."

"Learn what?" I said.

"Not to volunteer."

I smiled at him slightly. "Have a nice lunch," I said. The back of my neck itched.

The doctor is a handsome and gentle man. The women who come to him as patients especially like his deep, caring eyes. Sometimes a bolder woman tells me how she likes his gentleness.

Mai Yang arrived in the United States only last month. Her baby is due and she needs a doctor.

Mai is tall and very clean. She wears only a simply cut dress, coral-colored. It heightens the perfection of her skin and one forgets her swollen figure. Her face is serene and beautiful.

Most of the Vietnamese women wear their long hair rolled up in buns and twists at the back of their heads. Mai's raven black hair hangs straight, deliciously clean. It falls past her waist.

She isn't shy like the other Nam women. I take her into the exam room and we laugh over her language dictionary, trying to communicate by gestures and pointing at words. She gets across to me that she has had another baby, a boy, and that her first husband took the child.

When it comes time to undress there is no argument. I am sure we seem barbarians, but before I can explain to Mai or leave the room she removes her dress and stands unashamedly naked. I hand her a sheet to cover her and she calmly waits for the doctor.

I watch as the doctor talks to her, then listens to her heart and lungs. I can see her face while the doctor is at her back. Her skin is the color of amber velvet. He lifts her long, dark hair as if it were a sacred mantle - he is that gentle. Mai smiles. A beautiful, provocative smile.

Each time she comes I feel I know her though we cannot talk.

After the baby is born she returns for a check-up. She hands me the child, wrapped in a thick pink blanket. I take it in my arms carefully and go out of the exam room, leaving her with the doctor.

I marvel at the baby's likeness of Mai, pulling the blanket from the child fold by fold. It is as if the baby had no father, but only this perfect mother. Its hair is thick black around its small face. It yawns and its little rosebud mouth closes up tightly. It is dressed all in pink. Already Mai knows our girls are put in pink.

I hold the baby close. I touch the baby's tender cheek and watch as it searches instinctively for food.

***

The Vietnamese women no longer come to our office. The doctor has been in business for almost a year and has had too much trouble with the welfare women's cases and the government payments are far less than regular fee payments. The doctor cancels his agreement with the immigrant agencies and is relieved to lessen his problems.

But in the city streets I see the Vietnamese and Cambodian families walking. Some of the men I see with small new economy cars, their eyes looking from the window with small-wizened faces. I always slow my car to catch a glimpse of them.

I see two Asian men, dressed in dark wool suits that I'm sure they found at used clothing stores. They talk to each other in their native language, seem to be arguing as they stand behind a bus stop bench. I see a group of brown children playing tag with one another, and a little girl in a red coat holds tightly as a bigger boy, probably her brother, pulls her by the hand.

I look for a dirty yellow jacket sometimes, look carefully at the small women who have their hair piled on top of their heads. I look for a lithe woman with a long, full swatch of shining black hair.

The light turns red at Seventh East, near an Oriental Food market, and a small woman in a dark blue, mandarin collared jacket moves slowly along the sidewalk. Her hair is graying and she holds a tiny, round-eyed child's hand. I stare at her and she glances back at me, sees my eyes on her then lowers her gaze and smiles. Her hand goes to her mouth, covering the gaps in her smile where the teeth are missing. She picks up the child and turns its curious face toward me. I nod and smile and she nods to me, just as the light changes to green.

The Twisted Hair Saves the Day

The Beggar Woman and the Thief

There was once a blind woman who lived in the City of Peking. The modern name of this city is Beijing, but this is a story from olden times. She lived in the streets, having been blind from birth and left in the street to die.

An old woman had found the small child, taken pity on it and raised it as her own. When the old woman died, the child learned to fend for herself, singing for alms by the City Gate in the day and crawling between old buildings at night for shelter. Often as she sat at the gate many people would stop to hear her crying for alms, for her singing voice was very clear and piping as she sang chanting melodies that recalled for the people their own times of melancholy.

She earned enough money in this way to keep herself. She was able to buy small bits of cabbage and rice, and once in a while some rich merchant or lady would give her an old cloak or gown, thereby freeing themselves of their guilt for having such rich things when they caught sight of her.

When the girl was thirteen and begging in the streets she was caught off guard one day by an evil man. He, seeing her blindness, waited till night fall, then followed her as she picked her way carefully through the streets to the small crevice between buildings which she had called her home. There he beat her and raped her, pulling her hair and daring her to scream out for help. No one came. He used her over and over again, in all the most brutal ways he could think of, and then he took a knife, scraped it across her belly, laughing, saying loudly as he left her bleeding, "There, I have branded you a whore."

She did not move from this place for almost three days, so weak and beaten she was, and when she crept forth again she dared not tell anyone what had happened to her.

From then on, she was afraid when she walked the streets, fearing another man would touch her, would rip her clothes from her, use her and discover the scar she carried on her belly. She found too that she grew heavy with child, and she wept and mourned, knowing the cause of this new life. But when the child was born, a son, she took joy in it, knowing a kind of feeling she had never felt before, that of love. She kept the child close to her, taking it now to the market place, and to the City Gate. And the joy in her singing for alms increased so that her voice became excellent, so that many people came to listen to her, and each person who came dropped a coin at her feet, and many came close to her to tell her thank you. The alms she received became enough for her to find a small home to shelter herself and her son.

As her son grew, he learned to run errands for her, for he was not blind. He was a handsome child with a fine straight nose, clear almond shaped eyes and a mouth as pretty as his mother's, for his mother was beautiful, and even more beautiful because of her blindness, unaware that people often stared at her. As the son grew tall a shopkeeper offered to have him be apprenticed, and there the son went to live, leaving his mother alone again.

Now she sat at the City Gate and her song was often lonely, plaintive, but so very clear.

A thief came one day into the City of Peking disguised in the robes of a merchant. When he heard the woman singing, he crouched down for long hours, staring at her and listening to her music. Beneath his clothing, he held a dagger close to his heart, knowing always that he was in danger of being attacked. But this one time, sitting there on the open city street, he risked his life to listen to the woman.

Each day for a month he came to listen to her; he would drop her a coin, and sometimes he would stop her singing and ask her a question, almost whispering, so frightened she would become if he spoke aloud to her.

One afternoon still in full daylight, he followed her, for since she had been attacked she always stopped her singing early in the day, never trusting that a man would not follow her if she waited until nightfall.

The thief walked softly behind her at a distance and found she lived in one small room, lightless and without heat, which the shopkeeper who had apprenticed her son had given her. The thief stood in the doorless entry watching the woman move about in the dimness. She stopped and quietly listened, feeling his presence but hearing no sound.

"Who is there?" She asked, and the thief whispered as gently as he could. "So, this is how you live, woman."

"What do you want of me?" She asked, and retreated to the darkest corner of the room, recognizing the man's voice and thinking he meant to harm her as the other man had done.

He entered the room and sat down on the dirt floor which the woman had smoothed flat with her hands.

"I have listened to your music," he said. "And never have I felt so whole and clean. I only want to talk to you."

Then slowly, little by little, they began to talk, first haltingly and cautiously, but long into the night. The woman was startled by his words. She could not see his face but felt all the pain of his heart. He did not speak as the other street people did whom the woman often listened to, and he did not talk as the rich people who sometimes gave her their ragged gifts.

The timbre of his voice was rough, as though he had long fought for his life among wild men, but he spoke like a poet, with melody and rhythm in his voice. He told her many things that had happened to him, and sometimes she would hear his voice catch on a sob, but was unable, to see the bitter-hot tears that fell from his eyes. She knew too that he never reached a hand out to her, but only listened to her words and her songs, as she did to his. She never knew he was a thief, for he never told her, but he told her how his father had molested and beaten him one day, tried to kill the boy to cover his crime. His mother had taken him into the hills and left him there broken and bruised, expecting him to die, so that no one would know her shame. The man told her all these things, and in silence they sat together in sorrow.

The thief came home with her night after night, buying food for her and sitting long to talk. After many days, the thief told the woman he must return to the hills north of Peking where his home was. He did not tell her his home was a cave and that a large band of robbers, who were his men, were waiting for him there.

She felt a strange ache in her heart as he talked, and his urgency to leave left a deeper loneliness in her than she had ever felt. "May I touch you?" She asked him, and he took her hand and put it to his face. She ran her delicate fingers over his skin, memorizing every curvature, surprised at the harshness of the bones, for she imagined his face to be as soft as his heart. She felt his shoulders too, his waist, the entire length of his body, but never once did he try to touch her. He did not raise his hands, for he knew she would be frightened if he did so, and he had learned to love this woman with his soul as he never had another human being.

"I am sorry you must go," she said, and she knelt in front of him as he stood there and wept on his feet.

"Foolish woman," he said. "You cry too easily."

She shuddered and said, "I have learned to feel safe with you, but if you go, I will be afraid again."

He pulled the dagger from its hiding place over his heart, and pushed it into her hands. "You will put this over your heart, and you must use it if ever anyone tries to harm you again. I will return to you once a month and bring you money." And he lifted her from the ground and held her once before he went away.

Each day she sat by the City Gate to sing for alms, and once a month the thief came to her, each time dressed differently to disguise himself, but to her there was no disguise, for she recognized his voice immediately. He brought her not only money, enough to give her a good secure home and food and clothing, but he also brought her small gifts. Once a polished blood red stone which he found in the northern hills. She did not know what red was, but felt its jewel-like warmth in her fingers. Another time he gave her jade, pure clear green, which he told her was for healing. He brought her beads and told her a poem, one word for each bead, and he recited it with her until she could say it by heart. He brought her a woven blanket, made of the wool from sheep belonging to his tribesmen, and when he put it around her shoulders she promised him, "I will never be afraid again."

Then he was gone. He did not return to her for more than a hundred days, and she had no message from him, though he had left her enough money that she no longer had to beg. Still, on warm shining days, she would go to the City Gate and sit for an hour, singing her melodies in the sun. Her neighbors came and praised her and small children danced around her.

One day a new man came to her as she sat singing and said he had heard of her music. His voice was gentle, but she was so unused to speaking to strange men that she fell silent, her hand moving to her bosom. She felt the dagger the thief had given her for safety and comfort.

This new man was very rich. She could smell the perfumed oils he had used on his body. "Who are you?" She asked, and disguised her fear with scorn as the thief had taught her to do. The new man told her his story, how he had wandered many years and was looking for a place and a woman to make a home, and that in her music he thought he had heard the woman he could love.

"Do not mock me," said the woman, and when he said she was beautiful she answered, "Do not flatter me." But as the man talked she remembered the thief, and in this new man's voice she heard again a poet's song.

"I have a poem, a riddle, a friend I once loved sang to me. Listen, and if you can tell me the meaning, I will become your wife," she told him.

She began to sing, chanting over and over, and the wealthy man sat and listened and it seemed to him his own story in song. Her voice twisted the words, threw them into the air; over and over she sang, and she could not hear this man's weeping, for she could only see in her mind the face of the thief whom she trusted.

Once I slipped in a pond.
Once I died with my father.

I lost my soul and went wandering far
'Til I found you, singing at the Gate.
Your eyes could not see but your song
was so clear.
Your eyes could not tell you I am evil.
You listened to my song.
Once I slipped in a pond.
My mother could not save me.
Once I died a death for my heart died in
me.
You have given it back again
And I will always love you.

When she finished, many people stood around her, listening carefully, for she had never sung this song for them, and they marveled, saying it was the best she had ever sung. The wealthy man stood apart, silently weeping, and the woman cried out, "Sir! Are you still here, and can you answer the riddle. Do you know its meaning?"

He came to her side then, whispering just as the thief had done and speaking very carefully he said, "It is not a riddle you sing. It is my story."

"Not yours only," she said, "But many a man's. I will take your hand now, if you will walk with me."

The thief did not return, and the blind woman was very happy with this new man, for he was gentle and kind to her. She lived in a fine house with servants around her, and her son came to live there, working for his new father. But sometimes, when the moon was new, she asked her husband to take her to the courtyard to sit in the dark. She would put the warm brown woolen blanket around her, and she would ask him to point out where the moon would rise as a sliver and ask him to tell her how it looked. Then she asked to be left alone. She would pull from her robe the gifts from the thief, the red stone, the jade, the beaded necklace of the poem, and last of all, she would hold the dagger.

A Song for Sung Lien

In Memory of Louise Horntvedt Smith

Author's note: The story is based on the life of a Chinese girl who lived at the turn of the 19th century in the province of Sinkiang, China. Lien-Ehr is a diminutive form Of Sung Lien.

Book One

In the Children's Court

I

Sung Lien, come down from the tree. The lychee nuts you've thrown lie heaped upon the ground. I stand here laughing at the sight of you.

I will not tell our amah you have climbed up there in your peach colored gown. Come down Lien-Erh, and watch the cockerel strut beneath the bushes, looking for the nesting hens. Come down and watch his wide-legged walk.

II

See Naja, one-eyed snake, bloat his hood wide and sway for thee. Stay there, little sister, behind the skirts of amah's comforting wideness. Stay you there and safe from that venomnous branch.

III

If I dance for you, Sung Lien, will you watch me? I will imitate the wild boar rooting with his tusks. I will step his heavy body set upon his sticks. Around a pit I step for you. Around, around. Will you watch, sweet Lien-Erh, while I step around?

IV

Mother died while you yet required her milk. As daughters in a house with no mother longing after us, they said we are worthless. Then they set you in my lap and told me you would die unless I somehow learned to feed you.

I went out to the hills, sneaking out the side gate, Lien-Ehr, and found the goats an old man had left abandoned. I learned their milk is good. I separated the small Billy goat from its mother and struggled to bring the she-goat home for you. I tied it in the compound.

Let this thing be done, I said. Then returned to the hills and found the Billy goat. I set upon him and killed him, then fed his blood to you, mixed With his mother's milk.

So I lifted his life from him, sat you in my lap And spooned nourishment into your mouth.

This, Lien-Erh, happened before they allowed our old Amah to return to us. This happened when out father set us aside at our mother's death.

Ah, little one, you are too fair.
Someone may see your beauty and choose to turn you into a plaything for a man.
Please forgive me, Lien-Erh. I will take the juice of the betel nut and mix it with water, and every day before the sunrise, I will rub the juice into your skin. You will be dark, like the

hill people of the north. I hope that it does not penetrate into your soul. You must not be too comely. If your beauty should show, I fear for you, for you are small, no mother to watch over, a father whose only interest is his pipe, and his lithesome young wife. Your amah is so old she totters on her feet. What protection can she be to you?

If it is true, if they take you from me, then I must use every means to make you seem less than the precious gem you are. I must hide you, Lien-Ehr, as the lotus bud is hidden by its dark green covering. I would hide you beneath the darkest pond if I could, so that you would not find the pain at the hands of selfish men.

The sun rose for Sung-Lien.
The sun set for Lien-Erh.

Can I give you a magic trick? Can you pull a
rag of bright red silk From the old man's
sleeve?

See the magic in your two fingers as you sew.
See the little birds you weave in rose and
green. Set the needle down and lift the cloth
So you can see clearly. No matter, Lien-Erh.
The soil there from your finger prints,
Let me show you how to wash them.
The piece is good.

Presentation to the Grandmother

VI

Today, Sung Lien, I will twist your braids
gently and coil them each above your ears like
blossoms of the peonies. You have chosen the
red gown to wear. I am pleased.
Amah scolded me this morning.
She pulled my ear and said I must not make
believe that you are my child.
I am only your elder sister.

She reminds me that I am betrothed
and soon to leave you. That pains my heart,
for then, what shall become of you?

But today I will lift you up and present you
to the old Grandmother. She with the long
boney fingers was pleased to hear how I once
fed you the milk, mixed with the little he-goat's
blood.

I will carry you in, but I will set you down
upon the ground, and you must not fail to bow
to her, and do not stare too long at her, or at
once your bones will begin to grow brittle as
hers, and you will be old before you are a
woman.

You will not walk mincing. If the old woman is
pleased, I will play my flute for you, and you
shall dance. Remember to keep your feet
upon the ground, Lien-Ehr.

When we have left her chambers - and I know the old woman will bless you, then I shall tell you again how the stars fell one by one at your birth. How I saw the green feather of one star tracing behind the others, so that I knew God is with you.

Hurry now and find the gift
you are to take to the old woman.

VII

Now, Lien-Ehr, you must not be frightened. It is only the thunder. It is an old man walking. Lie here close beside me and look for the lightning. If you count slowly, he will tell you how far away his footsteps are. The time we have now is for our learning. You have shown me that our mother's death was another beginning.

The thunder grows louder. Count slowly
as I've shown you. E – er – san – ssu – wu.
He is five steps away.

Can you think of one good thing he brings in his basket? He brings water to make the bamboo glisten. I will tie one string of red upon your finger so you may have joy in growing things.

VII

The little sparrow you brought me is fading. It cannot live in such a small house as we have made for it. Can you set it free? Its wing is healed. The seeds we have gathered lie molding in the cage. The bird has no will to live inside his little home.

IX

Amah is scolding me again.

Today your father, though he would not call me to himself, sent message that my betrothal is complete. He set a seal upon a piece of silk and sent it to my husband's family.

Do not be concerned. Amah scolds, but I
know that secretly she is watchful, for you are
too small for anyone to take notice of.
Her eyes and mine watch over you.

Sung Lien, here is the flute our amah bought
from the old beggar in the market place.
It is one small gift for your seventh year.
Play for me the notes piping and clear.
Perhaps the little sparrow you set free
will come again to the window.

See the sunlight in the courtyard.
Let us play a shadow game. With each flute
note you give me, I will step from light to dark
and back again. There by the high wall is
where you first walked to me. You were no
bigger than the cockerel and yet you stepped
so well. Do you remember Qwan Yin of whom
I have told you? I left prayer beads beneath
my pillow last night and asked her to watch
over you.

In the night I dreamed you were made a slave. This I could not bear. Then I saw the goddess herself come down and lift you to her breast. She will not leave you to yourself.

Remember the dance I have made for you before, of the wild boar who circles and of the pit he digs. I will dance one more time and you must watch closely for in it lies your safety.

Look now to us, Quan Yin.
Your pale face I give reverence to.
See my small sister here, Sung Lien.
She has been a precious gift to me,
now I return that gift to you. Let her not die of loneliness. Let her not stand like one lonely willow. She is beautiful white jade and her heart is more rare than the mist of wild mountains.

I dance for Lien-Her. I become the wind.

I become the willow. Sell to me my sister, and I will pretend she is my slave.

Sung Lien, come, tie up my hair.
Learn to use the comb deftly and I will tell our amah. She must know my plan, and we will convince my father he has no need of your small presence.

Also, Lien-Ehr, you must pluck your eyelashes out and pretend to be a nervous child. This will not be easy. Your laugh is too like the song of water falling. But father never calls us for our company, so what does it matter. He will not recognize your nervousness is contrived.

Lien-Ehr, I will set you away from myself for a time to see if you remember my teachings. You must appear as a thing not worth having, else how will they allow me to buy my own sister?

It will happen as I have planned. They will announce the day chosen for my wedding and the old amah will begin to ask what things I may take with me.

Only three things do I want from this old man's house, and that is the red tablet that holds our mother's spirit, the seal my father set which is my name, and you, my little sister. Qwan Yin grant that this be true. The sun is upon Sung-Lien's brow, and hide as we might, her loveliness, the clarity of her skin shows through the continual staining I have done. Let no one here recognize the child.

Lien-Ehr, come here, sit beside me.
You must not push your feet up. Sit still.
Have you sewn in the new hemp seeds
the amah bid us carry? Have you drawn the
one character today I have shown you.
No, you may not laugh right now. See your
brother-cousins peering 'round the corner.

Sit still. If I am harsh with you, then you must
learn you are not a child much longer,
but a woman, and you come to act like one.

Show me your rice paper. Ah, it is rolled up
and pushed into your belt. Now I must show
you the proper place is in the sleeve. Do not
ask why this moment. Sit still and unfold it.
Show it to me as though I were your master.
Do not once lift your eyes to smile on me.

How weary I become. No matter, my wedding
day approaches and I beg Qwan Yin to watch
over us. If my husband is an awful man,
then I shall be done with any wishfulness.
If perhaps he is gentle, then I shall do all I can
to persuade him to buy my little sister also.

X

Sung Lien, do not mind now if I speak harshly.
It is for others' ears only, but you must appear
to be beaten. You must fall down and kowtow
whenever I look cross to you. Remember this,

you are the white rose-bud of my heart.

Bind up your feet. You are of an age to become like a woman. Do not wrap the bands too tightly. Already my feet ache more with remembrance of when I was like you. I will be stern. I am afraid you will be forgetful.

XI

Sung Lien, why do you lie there like a small sick bird? Do you dare not rise when I call you? Father has summoned us for his counseling. I am afraid of what he will tell me. Do not linger as though you were ill. You will not wear red on this day. I will choose for you as yet I have never done. You will wear this piece. It suits the sadness of my eyes.

Old amah whispers ugliness. Ah, Sung Lien, go to the window and tell me how the day will be.

Sung Lien must not hear me now. My father has already placed a price upon her head and mine. He has chosen to send me earlier to my new family; not even the words of the astrologers can dissuade him. He has put me away from him. Can I ever remember him touching me with kindness? Only once.

On my fifth birthday, he brought me a doll, small and exquisite, whiter than a pearl.
It was the same day I saw him raise his hand to my mother. She had said something that cut him to the heart, that I remember.
She said he had no care for anyone, but all things are as gold to him. If one thing weighed less than another, then it was of less worth to him. And she said she was as nothing.

All that day I listened to the stifled sobbing of my mother, and then he brought the gift to me, the lovely alabaster-white doll. It had painted eyes. Its hair was painted gold on its

head. The hands were as perfect as mine, but one of its miniature fingers was broken.
This was his gift.

Sung Lien, what do the clouds tell you?
Are they white, full with promise, or is there darkness and fear in them?

Sung Lien, come put your arms about my neck one more time. Know only this, that your heart lies in mine. If you prick you hand upon a needle, my hand bleeds. If your feet ache with the binding of woman's vanity, it is I who cannot walk for the pain.

Today the gown I put on you is dark green, your sash purple. My gown is white, for I am in mourning. Listen, the amah is coming.

Enter good old grandmother. How well you serve us. Would that I could cut my hair now and have done with living. Do not restrain Lien-Ehr. Today she will walk close beside me.

We have dressed her as plainly as we dare. Were my father to see my heart bleeding, surely he would be repulsed by my grotesqueness.

XII

The gray tiles are hard and cold, Sung Lien. Keep your back bent, your feet still. We are of least interest to our father. We will wait longer that the rest. Be still.

Father, I present myself to you in humility. As you wish, I walk to those places you have designated. I ask only that you allow those to go with me whom you have allowed to accompany me while I have lived in this household.

Oh my heart, dare you to bleed. Keep your silence, heart of mine.

Father, the little vermin you call my sister is fit for nothing but to be a serving maid, and inept at that. She will bring little or nothing in the market place. He dares to laugh. She is nothing to him, yet he beckons her to stand beside him. I have made her homely.

Oh, Qwan Yin, have you deceived my believing heart? Look how he touches her, as if she were something more to him than castaway daughter. His hand on her inward thigh, he turns her back to him and touches. If this very moment I had a knife, it would be the end of him. Do not allow his ugliness, Qwan Yin.

Father, you see, she has no eyebrows, no lashes. She has maimed herself by plucking at her hair. Her skin is very dark. She is nervous, always twitches. I have grown used to her.

What did the amah say? Did she say he had a young slave boy with him? She saw with her own eyes. Her eyes are dim. Yet what does he intend for my little sister?

The child is worthless sir, except that I have taught her to serve me a little. She could give comfort to me when I leave the warmth of your house. Yes, Father, I am to go to my husband's house with the new moon, as you prefer. Will you allow sir, the old amah to accompany me? And this small dingy child, sir, as my insignificant slave?

I cannot bow low enough to him, yet his eyes are caverns. They burn like coals. Has he a body I recognize? Did I issue out of those loins?

XIII

He detains the amah and Sung Lien in his court and puts me out. Yes, he says I am to leave, yet he gives no answer whether anyone shall accompany me.

The clouds thicken with the sunset. I can hear the distant old man walking with his thunder. Can I convince my heart to lie down like a dying bird? What purpose does he have for Lien-Ehr?

The old woman enters. Amah, old woman, you have deceived me. Where is my sister, Lien-Ehr, and why did he look thusly at her? Am I to go to my husband's house without Sung Lien or your assistance? How then can I hope to breathe?

Tell me one thing, Amah, will he let her come back into our rooms tonight? One time, will he let her come so I may whisper courage to her ear? She will be too faint-hearted. Have you seen her when the thunder comes? Her bones tremble inside her flesh, yet I was able to keep her from falling. What can he want of her? Amah, take her something tonight.

There is one small green stone. If she could
hold it she will know that I am with her.
If it is near her heart she will remember.
Take it and sew it into her clothing.
Take it and render the two of us as one.
Do not let her give up hope.

Gentle I must be with the night that rises in me. My hope is Lien-Ehr's only star. If I am hopeless, what can she become?

In the Husband's Court

I

Lien-Ehr, can you hear me whispering to you? I am borne away from you upon the backs of four black-skinned men. I could see them as their backs lifted me in the palanquin. As I dressed to leave our father's house I stood, my undergarments as white as a mourning gown, I wondered how my husband's family will greet me. I am told he is the elder in his house, his father, even as our mother, has gone to the ancestral home.

Little sister, listen to my whispering.
Somehow I am with you. Every night's sleep
you are close beside my bed. That envious old
man, our father, has kept you from me,
yet holds within his hands the goods my
husband's gold has brought him. My dowry
was a paltry thing, held in less than one hand,
so I cannot reckon what it is worth, my going
to this new man. I only hope that he is kind,
then I serve him with meek and grateful heart.
Yet one thing I must ask, that he allow my
little sister to enter here, even if as his slave.

Little sister, there is smoke in the street.
It is thicker than any clouds you and I have
witnessed and it is black. Though the curtains
are drawn about me, I can smell the tarry
choking odor. From the slit in the curtain I see
a charred house. The walls are blackened. I
wonder if the patriarch of that house is as evil
as our original home.

Walk with me, little sister. Invisibly step in my footprints. I will ask this new man to bring you back to me.

II

Three days I have been behind the walls of his house. The hours are long. Today is the wedding feast. I have not dared to look into the face of my husband. He greeted me when I arrived. My eyes downcast could only see the size of his feet, and I can tell you this, Lien-Ehr, his feet are small and fine for a man. He is not huge or old or ugly, as I had feared.

The maids are gentle, do not pull my hair, not like your little inexpert hands did. Yet how I miss your tugs at my hair, as though you always had hold on my heart. The maids hold up my arms and assist me. I am almost joyful, except for the lack of your presence. The women are with me every moment; thus I will not allow my tears to fall.

The mother of this house is kind. Her eyes are round. Thus I hope her son will appear to be. If I could speak, I would tell her about you. Little sister, are you well? Does the old amah snore still, and is she close beside you?

Now they lift my arms again and put on me the red wedding gown. My hands are twined in a length of silk and the headdress they put on me. You would laugh if you could see. You would call me red-dragon lady.

The veils allow me now to raise my eyes. I look to all the family members, judging more how they might accept you. How joyful I would be to see your betel nut-browned skin, to hear your tinkling laughter. You would run and dance and I would not have heart to stop you. Sung Lien, my heart cries out for you.

III

Sung Lien, do not forget your sister. The bridegroom stands beside me. He has the smell of sandalwood. The incense of the priests makes the air grow heavy. The priest has placed my hand in his. And though my hand is covered with its silken cloth, I feel warmth from him, his hand is soft. Though my head is bent, my eyes lowered, I know I am not like some brides. My wild heart beats, my heart aches for lack of your safety. I have stolen a forbidden look at the man who is to be my husband.

His jaw is not set. His eyebrows are not severe. Yet will I hope awhile for you. I will not stop trying to bring you home to me.
He and I share the alms cup together.
The wine is heated and my head grows light.
He touches silver chopsticks to my mouth.
Can I forget you ever, Lien-Erh?

IV

How difficult repose within his arms.
He sighs so gently I forget to be obedient.
Today he has asked if I know the characters

and whether I can read the classics.

The only brush strokes I know are the ones I taught you secretly, Lien-Ehr that I copied from the ancestral tablets, without permission. He has said he will set out to teach me and I am willing, little sister, even as you were with me.

Even in my joyfulness with him the shadow of memories plagues my eyes. He asks me why I mourn, when my time with him is so precious. What can I tell him? That our father is evil? He might not believe me; he himself is so kind. I told him your name, Lien-Ehr. He asked me so many question about you. I lost my voice when he asked me to describe you. Like a small sparrow, I said. Like a dancing cloud was all I could reply.

I do not know how to ask him to buy the child. His mother waits on me and does not ask me

To serve her. This I do not understand. She said a Buddhist monk came to her and said two stars would bless this house in the guise of one young woman. I do not understand.

V

The bamboo shoots of spring are pushing up in the courtyard by the fountain. Sung Lien, you should be here. Finally, I have asked my husband to inquire of you.

He has written a letter to my father, has enclosed a jade piece for my father's interest. Will our father's mind be generous? I dare not guess. This much I have prayed, that Qwan Yin be gracious to you, that you be not scarred within your soul.

I have a little dove, Sung Lien. My husband's gift to me, and on its foot a silken cord. I have dreamed of sending it to you. I have learned to write many characters and my brushstrokes write your name every day.

I have one more secret to tell you, little sister. I have happiness growing within me, and before a child is born in this house, I hope to have you with me. Have you forgotten me, Sung Lien?

Last night my husband called in musicians. They sat in the courtyard and gave us music. Under the stars, the smell of magnolia blossoms came so strong to me, yet there were no trees here. I felt your presence standing close behind me. When I turned, I saw the shadows move.

VI

Today is the feast of coming rain. A messenger was at our gate early, and I rose when the servant entered our room. He handed my husband our father's letter.
It said he has no need of you in his house, and if my husband was willing, he could buy you for a slave. The word he used to describe

you was 'simple woman.' Has he beaten you, Sung Lien? Or have you played the part I taught you? Never were you a simpleton.

My husband, how pleased I am now to be called his wife. He has procured my heart's longing. He says you may return to my side.

The gifts are made ready to buy you. He set them aside he tells me, before I first entered his room. He said his mother had cautioned him and that she had had a dream. Qwan Yin entered their red gate with her arms full. She carried one small child who had a maimed foot, and the young woman Qwan Yin led beside her was myself. My husband's mother, she is more mother to me than anyone I can remember, and she waits for you with eager heart. I have asked her what was meant by a child with a maimed foot, but she had no answer.

Perhaps, Lien-Ehr, when we are together, you can tell me all you have seen and felt since my leaving. My husband has lifted my heart. He says the cloud of darkness is lifted from off my shoulders. I ask him now what is in store for us.

VII

Bamboo is growing by our window. I asked my mother-in-law to accept my early coming into her room. I have many things to tell her.

Today we await your coming, Sung Lien, and before you arrive, I want to tell her our history. She listens as our mother once did to my dreams as well as my fear. I have told her how I once held you as a baby and she laughs when I tell her how you learned to walk and dance. She is so fearful that you will not like her, even as I was of her disliking me before I knew her. Her heart was lonely for a daughter, she has said, and I have brought her music she has never heard before. How good it is to be here.

VIII

With your arrival, Sung-Lien, I am all undone. See my hands flutter like my dove on its silken strand. Every time I hear a clatter in the streets, I run out or send my maid to see what the noise is.

The hours are longer on this day than on any other. Will I know your face? Have you changed so much?

Ah! Now the pounding on the gate is true, not only my imaginings. I must be composed but my feet cannot run quickly enough to see you walk in this courtyard.

My husband stands before me and my mother-in-law holds my hand still. Oh, to see your small face so wizened as the servant lifts the curtains for your descent.

Instead, two servants must assist you.
Why must they lift you as if you cannot walk?
Where are the feet of the little bird who
danced for me?

Like a one-legged ghost, the servants set you upon the ground. The cane you use makes you seem to be a little old man. Lien-Ehr, is this truly you? Your veil is lifted from your face. Your voice is too rasping for a child.
I know the worst has befallen you, but Qwan Yin has placed you in my arms.

My husband's anger I have never seen before. This is not how I left you. He wants to know what monstrous man was housed in the place of my father. I cannot tell him.

Forgive me, Lien-Ehr, for leaning on your slight frame and sobbing. To hold you alive is something I only dreamed of. You are taller, yet such a child, and you are no longer plump as you were when amah and I cared for you.

IX

This night is longer than daylight. I listen to you whisper your story before my husband and his mother. How could the man be so cruel to such an innocent one?

Again you ask for tea and rice and we watch you eat, amazed by your hunger. My husband has set your words down and tomorrow he calls the magistrate. What can one man do to another, when no outward law was broken?

To see your small frame was all I could ask, but to see you thus has caused us all to weep. My mother-in-law rises and folds another blanket about your shoulders, hoping to hold the chill of the night air from you. None of us want to leave you alone. The manner of your arrival this morning, Sung Lien, was something

I never expected. You came with not even one bundle of clothing and my husband has told me the cost was dear of sending for you.

We are bartered, sister, both of us, and tears become our only legacy. This man and woman who bought us, give us back our souls. And our once gentle natures may grow less suspicious than was our habit in our father's house.

Do you remember the boar's dance, little sister, how I said he danced upon his sticks? I did not know you would walk to me with such an injured leg.

X

My body thickens, Sung Lien.
Look how it is to become a mother.
My husband's joy is full, and mother-in-law is pleased. Should this child be a boy, I will teach him to walk like his father, but you, my

little sister, will teach him as I once taught you, and he will not be any less beautiful than you.

Sung Lien, look there! One star falls, then two and three. The feathered tail of the last star falling is all bright blue! I remember how you came to me with the heaven's promise. The comet's tail was green as jade. This child I will place in your arms has heaven's promise too.

Little sister, we must be quiet here. Remember how it was when the old man walked with thunder? I am afraid. It was so difficult to be separated from you. My heart fails in me to think this child may half relive the pain you have had to go through.

Afterword

The story is based on the life of the author's close friend, Louise Horntvedt Smith, who was still alive at the time the story was written. She died in 2010 from a series of strokes and the painful deterioration of her muscles and spine. She had requested that her body be cremated, which was done. Her husband reserved her ashes in a metal urn for three years and then asked the author to join him to scatter her ashes over her beautiful backyard garden. As the urn was opened, both her husband and the author were startled to find a small plastic bag atop the ashes. They each exclaimed, "I've never seen this necklace before!" As her husband took the necklace out of the bag they saw it was a fine silver chain with a tiny bird attached.

www.ingramcontent.com/pod-product-compliance
Lightning Source LLC
Chambersburg PA
CBHW061028100726
47911CB00001B/10